SUZY,
LED ZEPPELIN
AND ME

Fantasy | Sci-fi

ARTIN

ZEPLIN AND ME

FICTION

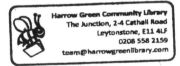

SUZY,
LED ZEPPELIN
AND ME

Martin Millar

Suzy, Led Zeppelin and Me
by Martin Millar

Published in 2002 by
Codex Books
PO Box 148, Hove, BN3 3DQ, UK
www.codex-books.com

ISBN 1 899598 22 7

Designed and typeset by
Surface Impression Ltd

Printed in the UK by Bookmarque Ltd

one

ON THE 4TH OF DECEMBER, 1972, Led Zeppelin came to play in Glasgow. If you live outside of Britain, you might not know where Glasgow is. It's a large city on the west coast of Scotland. Scotland is just north of England.

I won't trouble you with any more geography. I know you have a short attention span. So have I. I don't seem able to watch a programme on TV for more than a few seconds without changing channels. I can't sit through long films any more. I never go to the theatre for fear of being bored. When I'm reading a book I need the chapters to be brief.

No part of this novel is longer than a few hundred words. Even with a short attention span, you'll be able to read it easily, a little at a time.

It mostly concerns events surrounding the Led Zeppelin gig, all those years ago. I remember the main events well but my memory for detail can be poor. This often causes me problems. I never remember who people are if I've only met them a few times, or when anyone's birthday is, or the date I'm meant to do anything. So I've been asking old friends about the concert, finding out things I might have forgotten. For instance, was it raining on the night of the gig? Glasgow is a fairly wet city and it could well have been raining, but I can't remember. And where did the young women at my school buy their afghan coats? I must have known that at some time. I can still remember how to slit a pair of jeans to the knee, and sew in a triangle of bright material to give them an 'extra-flared' look.

My friend Greg was there, and Cherry, and Zed, and also Suzy, who was Zed's girlfriend some of the time.

Greg was in love with Suzy, and so was I, or so it seemed at the time. I was fifteen, and easily confused about emotions. I was feeling passionate all through the autumn and winter; passionate about Suzy, and Led Zeppelin.

I see that this chapter is just 377 words long. Short enough even for your limited attention span. You can't argue with that.

two

MOST OF THIS BOOK is a record of conversations between myself and my friend Manx. Even when I haven't bothered writing it down so it looks like a conversation, or put quotation marks round the text, it's most probably something I've been talking to Manx about.

The title of this novel could have been *Conversations with my Friend Manx*. That would have been a good name for a book. Snappy and accurate. But I rejected it because I wanted to have 'Led Zeppelin' in the title. After all, that is what this book is mainly about, me going to see Led Zeppelin when I was at school and telling my friend Manx about it a long time afterwards.

I am very fond of Manx. She's always prepared to listen to my Led Zeppelin stories. I talk to her every day, usually on the phone. Other times we email each other. Sometimes we meet, but since Manx had her baby she finds it difficult to make arrangements. Despite the high quality of my Led Zeppelin stories, Manx is frequently depressed. She's been depressed since she had the baby. I intend to cheer her up. It's my mission in life.

"So," says Manx, "were you there on that day in 1972 when Led Zeppelin came to Glasgow?"

"I certainly was, Manx. And I'll tell you all about it. I will tell you about it in a manner similar to the way Plato tells his readers about Socrates in *The Symposium*, which is a very interesting book, relating all manner of things through the person of Apollodorus, who heard about it from Aristodemus."

"That's fascinating," says Manx. "But don't get carried away. Your Ancient Greek stories were last year. This year it's Led Zeppelin."

Socrates, who lived around 400 BC, still makes the occasional appearance in the modern world. Only a few years ago he featured in a film, *Bill and Ted's Big Adventure*. I enjoyed that. I liked Bill and Ted. They would have loved the Led Zeppelin gig.

three

A YOUNG FRIEND OF MANX'S recently celebrated her twenty-first birthday. We watched as she and her friends went off to enjoy themselves.

"I wish I was twenty-one," said Manx.

"Me too," I agreed.

It made me wonder what I did for my own twenty-first birthday. I can't remember. My mind is blank. What did I do? There must have been some sort of festivity.

I was fifteen when I saw Led Zeppelin. I remember that well. I left home when I was seventeen. I remember that. But my memories of four years later are less clear.

I am now just past forty. Too young, I hope, for senile dementia. Perhaps I don't remember things I don't want to remember. Perhaps my twenty-first birthday celebration was a flop. Maybe nobody came.

I have rarely enjoyed birthdays. I distinctly recall

some depression on my sixteenth when I felt that I was getting old. A year before that, when Led Zeppelin were coming to town, everything was young and exciting, and the nagging unhappiness caused by my passion for Suzy was not yet causing me serious problems.

A friend in Glasgow tells me that he can't remember very much about the gig. He doesn't know if it was raining that night but he does recall that it was very cold outside. When we came out of the auditorium you could see clouds of steam rising off people's bodies. After the excitement of witnessing Led Zeppelin playing on stage only yards away from us, everyone was drenched in perspiration and the warmth of our bodies sent vapour flying away into the freezing night air.

Late into the night, I sometimes search the internet for the names of people I used to know when I was at school, even though there is little chance that I would ever want to talk to any of these people again. I'm not certain why I do this. Probably it is a symptom of my dissatisfaction with life. I am always dissatisfied with something or other. I always have been. The only time I can remember being totally satisfied was when Led Zeppelin walked on stage and started playing. They played for two hours. Two hours of complete satisfaction. You can't argue with that.

Many years later, I'm living in London, making a living as a writer. I've progressed far enough to be judging literary competitions. But more of that later. Now I should tell you a little bit about my friends at school; Greg, and Suzy, and maybe Cherry, though Cherry was of not much account. And I will also say more about Suzy's boyfriend Zed who was, crucially, a year older than us. Greg and I liked Zed. We looked up to him though it was annoying that he was going out with Suzy, who we were both in love with.

I wasn't at Suzy's twenty-first birthday party but I'm sure it was a fabulous celebration. She was the sort of person who would always have fabulous birthday celebrations.

four

"So," says Manx, "tell me about the girl you were in love with at school. Were you continually making a fool of yourself about her?"

"I don't think so. I guarded my emotions quite well. Anything else would have been fatal. You know how mean kids are to each other."

Suzy was in the same class as me at school, but as I was fifteen and she was sixteen it was hopeless being in love with her. Sixteen-year-old girls don't go out with fifteen-year-old boys. Undoubtedly you will have experienced this at some time in your life. If you are male, you will remember looking longingly, and hopelessly, at a girl in school who was just older than you but might as well have been on the cover of *Vogue* for all the chance you had of ever going out with her. And if you are female, I expect you remember some boy who often looked at you in an odd way, and who, though you didn't really mind him, you would rather have died than been seen on a date with.

"Such is life at that age," says Manx.

I nod.

Now I'm past forty, no one would refuse to go out with me merely on the grounds that I was a year younger.

"A woman might have plenty of other reasons, like my poor track record in relationships for instance, but age wouldn't enter into it."

11

I can still feel some slight humiliation that girls in my own class at school looked down on me as immature. They were right. Compared to them I was.

five

I WAS NEVER VERY HAPPY AT SCHOOL. I'm not sure why. Looking back, it doesn't seem that anything particularly bad was happening. But when you are twelve or thirteen, just not getting on with the teachers can be enough to make you unhappy.

I didn't have many friends apart from Greg. We didn't like sports and we didn't watch much TV and we didn't seem to have anything to talk about to the other people in our class. Our hair and our hippy clothes got Greg and me laughed at everywhere. I never had a girlfriend. Until I was thirteen or so I didn't really realise that boys had girlfriends. I was shocked when I saw some boys I knew going around with girls. I seemed to have missed out on this stage of development.

"You think we should get some girlfriends?" I said to Greg, trying not to sound too serious.

"Sure," said Greg.

We couldn't think of much else to say on the subject. Neither of us knew how to get a girlfriend. We were out in the early morning darkness, delivering newspapers, and carried on in silence up the street.

"Who would you want to go out with?" asked Greg eventually, folding a copy of *The Scotsman* prior to cramming it through a letterbox.

I shrugged, implying that I had not yet given the matter enough thought to make a final decision. That was untrue. I already knew that if I was to have a girlfriend, the number one candidate would be Suzy. She lived not far from me, just up the hill. I often met Suzy as we walked to school and we were in the same class for most subjects.

I didn't like to mention her name to Greg in case he laughed at me for pitching my ambitions too high. After all, Suzy was nine months older than me, and at age thirteen, this was already starting to tell. I was still childlike, still playing games. Suzy had suddenly become a young woman, with cosmetics, new clothes, new attitudes and, quite noticeably, a new shape.

"Suzy's nice," said Greg, taking me by surprise. It was troubling that he had already noticed her.

"You think so?"

"Of course," said Greg. "She's a ride."

At our school in Glasgow that was a way of expressing approval. It was certainly graphic enough.

We didn't deliver a newspaper to Suzy's house, but after this we would always stare wistfully at her bedroom window as we passed.

A month or so afterwards, I asked Zed what he thought of Suzy. He shrugged, implying that he thought nothing at all of Suzy. That was quite treacherous, in retrospect, as he ended up going out with her and causing me a lot of distress, but really Zed had no reason to share his thoughts with me. He was a year above me at school. That counted for a lot.

I'm not going to say much about school. After all, you were at school. You know what it's like. But you might not know what it's like to be at school when Led Zeppelin are coming to play in your city, as they were in Glasgow, in 1972.

SIX

GREG AND I WERE DEPRESSED when Zed started going out with Suzy. Often in the dark evenings, standing on street corners with nothing to do, we'd complain about it.

"It's all right for Zed," we'd say. "Suzy doesn't mind going out with him. He's a year older."

"If we were a year older she'd go out with us."

In reality it was not just Zed's age which entitled him to his position as boyfriend to the very desirable Suzy. Zed was high up among the coolest people in our school. In the early seventies he would turn up for classes in an afghan coat, sometimes even wearing beads. Teachers would complain about the length of his hair, and he'd look at them blankly through a pair of blue-tinted John Lennon glasses.

Zed was far too cool to be friends with me. His other friends never spoke to me at all. It was beneath their dignity. But Zed didn't seem to worry about things like that. We lived fairly close to each other and if we met on the way to school he would always be amiable.

We liked the same sort of music. Neither of us had any doubt that the best band in the world were Led Zeppelin. Not only were Led Zeppelin the best band that existed, they were the best band that could possibly exist. If somewhere in the universe there was a Platonic ideal form for a band, a perfect band of which all others could only be a pale reflection, then it was Led Zeppelin.

There were no arguments about this in 1972 and I'm not going to get into any arguments about it now. Led Zeppelin were the best band, and that was that.

If Greg and I were not cool enough to be potential boyfriend material, we were at least able to visit Suzy as friends, drinking tea, listening to records, and talking. Sometimes Suzy would talk about her ambitions.

"I've decided to study at university and be a doctor."

Greg and I were impressed.

"Don't you have to study for a really long time?"

Suzy nodded. As a girl with ambition, she didn't mind the prospect of lengthy study.

"I want Zed to go to university too," she continued. "But he keeps saying he wants to travel to India."

This was quite a popular thing to do in those days but it was obvious that Suzy disapproved. It sounded like an exciting idea but I remained silent, not wishing to contradict her.

Suzy, she was beautiful in her love beads and her afghan coat, which was light brown with green embroidery, with white fur round the edges. She had a bag made of leather patches and platform boots made of denim. She had feline features and long blonde hair, very bright. Bright blonde hair was not that common in Glasgow, the Scots being predominantly dark-haired. My own hair was blond, though not as bright as Suzy's. I used to sit behind Suzy in class, just staring at her hair. So did Greg. We had not yet sorted out the difference between love and lust, which was understandable. We were only fifteen. Plenty of people never sort that one out.

Greg was a good musician and wondered about joining a band, although that seemed to be a difficult thing to do. In 1972 everyone thought you had to start playing guitar when you were very young and be a highly proficient musician before you could join a band. This changed in 1976 when punk rock made it a decidedly positive thing not to be a very good musician. One day people picked up guitars for the first time and the next day they walked on stage in a band. This was a much better arrangement.

Today anyone can join a band even if they can't play music at all, just so long as they can work a sampler, or a computer, and this is a much better arrangement as well. It was a dull idea that young people had to be expert musicians before they could climb on stage and get rid of their angst and their frustrations through music. Anyone should be able to do it.

So Greg wondered about being in a band, but thought he would probably end up studying English at university and maybe getting a job somewhere after that. I had no ambitions. I have never had any ambitions.

seven

HERE IS HOW I FIRST SAW MANX. In 1985, which was thirteen years after the Led Zeppelin gig, I was sitting on a bus at the traffic lights when a young woman in a Nefertiti hat walked across the road.

I was on a 159 bus in Brixton Road. Brixton is in South London and the 159 is my favourite bus. Then, as now, the buses on the 159 route were old routemasters with the open door at the back. Routemasters are comfy old-fashioned buses, first manufactured in 1935. The door at the back is always open so you can leap on and off at traffic lights. They still have a conductor and they're a nice curved shape. Many people like these old buses best, but they're being phased out these days in favour of one-man-operated buses, which are ugly and square.

The one-man-operated buses can let you on and off if you're in a wheelchair. So I suppose they are a good thing really. But I will miss the old buses when they disappear completely.

The 159 is a very useful bus. It runs from Streatham down the hill to Brixton and Kennington, over the river to Trafalgar Square and right up to Oxford Street. It used to go to Baker Street, before they shortened the route. Baker Street is where Sherlock Holmes was supposed to live.

When the young woman walked past, I couldn't help but be impressed. Her hat was an extravagant garment that took confidence to wear. It stood up eighteen inches from her head like a long black pill box, an angular, brimless version of a top hat, but prettier. It was a copy of the famous hat worn by Queen Nefertiti in ancient Egypt and it was a very unusual thing for anyone to be wearing in 1985, even in Brixton, which had always been relaxed in its dress codes.

She had light brown skin, and was what I had learned to call 'mixed race'. I say 'learned to call' because when I was growing up in Glasgow I would have called anyone with one black parent and one white parent 'half caste'. That's what anyone in Glasgow in the early seventies would have said, without ever thinking that anybody might object. No one there had ever heard the term 'mixed race'. Looking at the phrase 'half caste' now, it seems strange. Half of what? What does caste have to do with it?

The girl in the Nefertiti hat breezed down the road as if it was the most natural thing in the world to be walking along Brixton Road in her outlandish headgear, and a long robe, which may well have been a copy of the robe Queen Nefertiti wore 3,300 years ago in Egypt.

I was impressed. I still am. I thought about the young woman in the hat for a long time after that, and I always wondered if we would meet. It would have been a big surprise to me then if someone had told me I would one day be judging a literary competition with her.

I was a shockingly bad judge in that competition. I am ashamed when I think about what a useless judge I was. No one would ever ask me to judge a literary competition again.

eight

ZED, SUZY, GREG AND I all lived quite close to each other in Bishopbriggs, a large collection of semi-detached houses on the northern edge of Glasgow. Cherry lived nearby as well, although we didn't see her so much at school as she was a year younger than us. This suited Greg and I just fine. Cherry had red hair, freckles, glasses and, worst of all, still wore a school blazer, even though we were no longer obliged to do so. Cherry was what would later be described as a nerd. If Greg and I saw her coming while we were walking to school, we'd accelerate so she couldn't catch up with us, even when she shouted for us to wait.

Greg and I were both aware that we were not a very cool pair of kids ourselves We took a fair amount of mockery at school. We had no desire to make things worse by associating with Cherry. She was the sort of person who always did her homework and was liked by the teachers. It annoyed us that Suzy was friends with her.

"Why," wondered Greg, "does Suzy bother with her?"

"Their parents know each other. And they live right next door to each other."

Greg pulled at the ends of his hair, making a mental calculation as to its length. We both had very long hair. I was always getting in trouble at school about it, and so was Greg. Only a few years before, no male in Glasgow would have had long hair, and teachers were still finding it distressing that their charges were now turning up to school with hair flowing over their shoulders.

Not only our teachers objected to this. Many citizens of Glasgow found it hard to take. 1967 and the era of the hippies had made little impression here and in 1972 Greg and I were routinely abused in the street because of our hair.

Zed's hair was particularly fine. It was curly, and made him look a little like Marc Bolan.

"It's no wonder Suzy goes out with him," Greg and I would say, musing on the iniquities of life. "He looks like Marc Bolan."

Marc Bolan was the singer in T Rex. We didn't like T Rex because they were too poppy, which, for a band, was the ultimate crime. Back in the days of progressive rock we were very serious about things like that. Led Zeppelin never put out singles because singles were too poppy and we understood that completely. But we couldn't deny the effect that Marc Bolan had on women.

Zed was like that. He was our local Marc Bolan. He loved Led Zeppelin with a fierce passion.

nine

CHERRY WAS AN IRRITATING GIRL. The red hair, freckles and glasses with black plastic rims were bad enough, but she was also extremely clever and that was annoying. Even though she was a year below Greg and me, she knew more about school work than we did.

When we were baffled by algebra or calculus Cherry would know how to do it even though her class hadn't reached that level yet. She'd been reading the books in her own time and working things out for herself before her teacher explained them. Although this was useful when we needed help with schoolwork, it wasn't something that Greg and I could easily forgive.

We'd run into her on the way home from school. Invariably she would be walking home alone.

"How do you do this equation?" we'd ask. Or, "how do you find out stuff about Egypt?"

We always seemed to be doing projects about Ancient Egypt. Our teachers were obsessed with the place.

Cherry would tell us how to do the equation or how to find out information about Egypt and we'd scribble down a few notes then walk on quickly and leave her behind. If Cherry tried to keep up, we'd tell her to go away and stop bothering us.

"What a loser," Greg would say, when she was still within earshot.

"She really loves it that she knows all these answers. It's because she's always sucking up to the teachers."

Apart from Suzy, who didn't really like her that much, Cherry's only friend was Phil. Phil lived nearby and he was universally despised because he was overweight and went to a special school for clever adolescents. Even though Greg and I knew what it was like to be picked on and should have known better, we were mean to Phil. We couldn't resist it. His parents were a little wealthier than the rest of the residents and Phil always managed to wear clothes which somehow looked both too expensive and too childish for his age. Besides, he was fat, which seemed like a substantial crime. If we met Phil in the street we'd laugh at him. Phil would ignore us. Occasionally he'd visit Cherry.

"There goes Cherry's boyfriend," Greg would say, and we'd laugh at the thought of them going out together.

Phil rarely left his house in the evenings, so Cherry never had anyone for company. Greg and I hung around in the park or walked to the shops to buy cigarettes with the money we earned delivering papers. Sometimes we'd run into Zed, who'd sometimes have some alcohol which he'd share with us. We had no sympathy for Cherry.

"You can't expect to have any friends if you wear glasses like that," said Greg, and I agreed. I was meant to wear glasses myself but I almost never did. Life was difficult enough without adding to my problems by wearing glasses.

Cherry kept a diary, another bad thing. Sometimes she could be seen on her own at school, scribbling down an entry. Only a person who really didn't a have a life would do that.

Cherry went to violin lessons. She kept a diary. She didn't even know who Led Zeppelin were. What a loser.

ten

LED ZEPPELIN were by far the most successful rock band of their time. They ruled the world from 1969 till 1976 and released a series of albums that sold in enormous numbers. They didn't go out of style till the arrival of punk rock. When the furore of punk had died away, they worked their way back up in public esteem until it was quite normal to hear contemporary rock musicians talk about them as a major influence. They broke up in 1979 when John Bonham died. He was their drummer and he choked to death on his own vomit after a heavy drinking session. After this they didn't want to carry on.

Manx is not that impressed with any of this.

"Who cares nowadays?"

"Well, I don't know if anyone cares, Manx. But if no one cares, so what? I can still write about it."

Manx shrugs. She's feeding Malachi so is not able to devote her full attention to the conversation.

When I originally set out to write about Led Zeppelin I assumed that their name would still resonate for most readers. I noticed that when Otto, the bus driver in *The Simpsons*, was about to drown in an episode only a few years ago, his last words were "Zeppelin Rule." But maybe Manx is right. Perhaps the band is no longer that familiar. Rock music itself is no longer so prevalent as it used to be. Techno and dance music has been popular for a long time and a whole generation has grown up divorced from the Led Zeppelin mythos not just by time, but by genre. There must be many people to whom Led Zeppelin is nothing more than a name from the distant past.

Malachi finishes feeding.

"Good baby," says Manx, and rocks him around a little. Malachi gurgles with pleasure.

"Are you going to go on and on about why Led Zeppelin were so great?" asks Manx.

"Not really. That would be tedious. I'm long past the stage of trying to persuade people about politics, religion, or the great mysteries of the universe, so I'm not going to try and persuade anyone about the merits of a rock band. It doesn't matter to me if anyone thinks they were good or not. They only have to appreciate how great we thought they were at the time, and that was as great as a band could be."

We didn't really count them among the ranks of mortal men. They were more akin to mighty gods from Valhalla, come down to Earth to raise hell. They were so important to my life that I bought two of their albums before my family had a record player. I used to walk around the playground at school, carrying them under my arm. I wasn't the only person to do this.

"So," says Manx, "were they the biggest influence on your life?"

I think about this. Malachi, sitting on Manx's knee, is still looking happy.

"Well probably not. The Sex Pistols probably had more influence. Punk rock was very liberating, and the Sex Pistols were a great band. But they weren't as good as Led Zeppelin, and anyway, when the Sex Pistols arrived I wasn't fifteen any more, or a virgin, or living at home. I wasn't quite so dependent on music to rescue me from life. After I moved to London, if life was tough I could go into a bar and get a drink. Back at school if things were bad there was only Led Zeppelin."

Led Zeppelin were too important ever to come and play in Glasgow. I couldn't believe it when the gig was announced. I got out my copy of *Led Zeppelin Two*, studied the mighty Zeppelin that flew across the gatefold sleeve, and wondered if it was possible.

eleven

MANX HAS NOT BEEN HAPPY since she had her baby.

I'm talking to her on the phone. She's telling me about her new cosmetic, Estée Lauder Uncircle, which is eye treatment for dark circles. Recently she's been looking tired.

"I have to get rid of the dark circles before I can try my new Lancôme Masquisuperbe All Over Face Glow. No use having a glowing face if I've got huge shadows under my eyes."

I can see her point. Manx is keen on make up. She doesn't like it that she's looking tired. When she's pushing the baby around in his pushchair, she wants to look glamorous, and failing that, at least healthy.

We talk about make up for a while till Manx changes the subject and asks me about my Led Zeppelin book.

"Is it a rock biography?"

"No, it's a novel. But it includes lots of true things. Like the girl I was in love with at school and stuff like that. She had long blonde hair and her father was a manager in an insurance office. She used to wear Mary Quant lipstick. Mary Quant was still a big name in cosmetics at the start of the seventies."

Manx is distracted by some baby noises. When I first met her, Manx had a temporary job taking money at a theatre in the centre of London. At that time she told me she was a lesbian, and had a steady girlfriend. After a while she broke up with her girlfriend, declared herself bisexual, and we went out for a while. We became close but the relationship just petered out, as all my relationships do. Fortunately, we remained friends. We are better friends now than we ever were when we were going out with each other.

After we broke up, Manx had a few more affairs with young men before deciding she liked women better. A year or two after that, she became friends with a man who was gay. They started living together and had a baby. Then he decided that really he was gay, and left her for a man he met in a supermarket. All this would have surprised me at one time but I'm used to it now.

Manx emerged with a baby and a bad case of depression. She is proving very resistant to being cheered.

I describe my Led Zeppelin book.

"I'll have to change a few names of course."

Manx asks if she will be in it and I tell her that yes, she probably will be.

"Don't mention that I was using cocaine till the third month of pregnancy."

I promise not to. I thought it was a fine effort to give up for the last six months. Or the last four and a half months, the baby being a little premature.

"How is judging the literary competition going?"

"Very badly," I admit. "I haven't read any of the books yet. In fact, I haven't opened the box they came in. It's still right behind the front door. It's been there for three weeks. I'll do something about it soon."

The baby starts howling and Manx has to end the conversation. I think about the literary competition. I wish I hadn't become involved. Why did the British Council ask me to be a judge of their New Fiction competition? I haven't read a novel published by anyone born in the twentieth century since they made me read them at school, and even then I wasn't paying attention. I was too busy thinking about Suzy, and Led Zeppelin.

Suzy was so beautiful and so alluring. At times it seemed to Greg and me that we had been specially blessed to have her living nearby. But at other times it seemed like a curse. I would get so unhappy watching her walk down the street and knowing that I had so little chance of ever making any impression on her. During those times there was nothing to do but listen to Led Zeppelin and wait to get older, when things might improve, though I wasn't convinced that they ever would.

twelve

Here is the set list from Led Zeppelin at Green's Playhouse:

Rock and Roll
Over the Hills and Far Away
Black Dog
Misty Mountain Hop
Since I've Been Loving You
Dancing Days
Bron-Y-Aur Stomp
The Song Remains the Same
The Rain Song
Dazed and Confused (Including The Crunge)
Stairway to Heaven
Whole Lotta Love (Including Everybody Needs Somebody to Love, Boogie Chillun, Let's Have a Party, Stuck on You, I Can't Quit You)

First Encore:
Heartbreaker

Second Encore:
Immigrant Song
Communication Breakdown

What a fine set. Pummelling heavy metal, melodic Celtic whimsy and tortured electronic blues. Great songs, loud guitars, and a load of weird noise. I loved loud guitars and weird noise.

"You know Manx, if anyone had said to me when I was at school, 'Led Zeppelin are terrible, you should listen to Elvis Presley instead,' I would have mocked them. So I'd never try and tell anyone that Led Zeppelin were better than their favourite band of the moment. You can't go around listening to music that your parents liked. Anyway, I like to hear new music myself. But I must admit there have been times, when I've been watching some bunch of fumbling indie kids droning on about nothing very much on stage, when I'd have been pleased if a huge time warp had opened up and the mighty Led Zeppelin had marched into the auditorium.

"That's what a fucking guitar is meant to sound like," I'd say, and dare anyone to contradict me.

The appearance of Led Zeppelin in Glasgow at Green's Playhouse was the highlight of my entire life in Scotland.

"Do you wish you were there now?" asks Manx.

"What? Fifteen years old and going to see Led Zeppelin in the same year that 'Stairway to Heaven' was released? Of course I wish I was there now."

"I wouldn't mind being there myself," says Manx, who is struggling with her computer project, and wondering how to pay her telephone bill.

thirteen

THE ADVERT ANNOUNCING THE LED ZEPPELIN TOUR took me by surprise. The tour started in Newcastle and the third and fourth dates were to be in Glasgow. I stared at it suspiciously. It seemed unlikely to be true. Could it be a misprint? Led Zeppelin had never played here before. They were too important to come to Glasgow.

Green's Playhouse was a venue which bands visited regularly. I'd already seen other groups there; progressive rock stalwarts of the day such as Hawkwind, the Who,

Mott the Hoople, Emerson Lake and Palmer and Captain Beefheart, but Led Zeppelin? Surely not. They were busy in Valhalla. It was possible that they might descend to play a few important dates in the USA. I could even imagine them visiting London. But Glasgow? It was hard to believe.

The advert stated that tickets would go on sale all over the country at 9am on Friday the 10th of November. I called up Greg.

"Do you think they'll really come?"

"Of course," said Greg. "Why wouldn't they?"

I couldn't really explain why I thought they wouldn't. After all, it said so clearly enough in the music paper. I didn't want to admit that I felt so insignificant in the world that it seemed to me unlikely that Led Zeppelin would find it worth their while to play in any city I lived in.

Possibly they didn't know I was actually in Glasgow. If I kept a low profile, everything might turn out all right. I would see Led Zeppelin.

"It'll be great," said Greg. "We'll see Robert Plant and Jimmy Page and they'll play 'Stairway to Heaven' and 'Whole Lotta Love' and everything –"

"It'll be fantastic."

Overwhelmed by the prospect, Greg started chanting the riff to 'Whole Lotta Love' down the phone and I sang along with him.

We'd started going to concerts when we were twelve. Green's Playhouse was not licensed to sell alcohol, which was fortunate for us as Glasgow was a tough city in which to enter a licensed venue if you were underage. If Green's Playhouse had had a bar I'd never have seen any of those bands.

People used to persuade older brothers, older friends or, in an emergency, complete strangers, to buy alcohol for them and then drink at a furious pace between the bus stop and the venue. I assumed that this was normal behaviour all over the country.

It was some weeks till the tickets were due to go on sale and from the moment the advert appeared, I did not feel entirely sane. I'd find myself trembling, or distracted, or sweating, or just staring into space. School, which was generally bad, became worse. I couldn't concentrate on my work. I was too busy worrying that I might have a road accident and not be able to queue up for a ticket.

It was difficult enough coping with the Led Zeppelin frenzy. When Suzy turned up at my house one day, wearing a cheesecloth shirt that strained at its buttons, and said that she was unhappy with her boyfriend Zed, it seemed like too much to bear.

"Are you queuing overnight for a ticket?" she asked me, and I replied that I was. There was no chance of getting one otherwise.

"Me too," said Suzy. "We can queue together."

A vivid image of me sheltering Suzy beneath my army greatcoat, keeping her warm in the queue, settled down on me, and remained there for a long time.

Greg was already in my room. He gave up the only chair to Suzy. I liked it better when Suzy was sitting. Although I would not come right out and admit it, I suspected that she was an inch taller than me. I was already disadvantaged by the age difference and the lack of coolness on my part. If it was ever proved that I was actually shorter than Suzy, there was not much point in going on with things. I might as well just wear a sign saying 'small guy, will never have a girlfriend'.

I lit some incense, a habit both Greg and I had picked up from Zed. On hearing Suzy's complaints about her boyfriend, Greg and I were nervous. We had reason to be. The last time we had been at Suzy's house she had done something which more or less picked up our world and turned it on its head. Leaving her house via the kitchen, after saying goodbye to her mother, Suzy had poured a glass of water, hurriedly taken a small packet of pills out of her bag and popped one into her mouth. They were contraceptive pills. Greg and I were astonished, though we tried not to let it show. It had never occurred to us that any girl we were friends with might actually be taking contraceptives and, by strong implication, having sex.

So there we were in my room. Suzy was dissatisfied with her boyfriend Zed. She was taking contraceptives. I was aware of my ignorance about the female sex drive. I had some sort of idea that taking the pill might make women lose control of themselves and just have to fuck someone. What if she had an uncontrollable desire to have sex with someone right now? Would it be me or Greg? If I had to look the other way while Suzy climbed into bed with Greg right underneath my Led Zeppelin poster, I really wasn't going to be very happy about it.

"I met a guy at the university," said Suzy. "He asked me out. What do you think I should do?"

I crashed back to reality. Suzy wasn't about to fuck us after all. She wasn't going to ditch Zed for either of us. She was going to ditch him for someone at university, someone older and, no doubt, even more hip. She was about to drift even further out of our reach.

"I don't trust students," I said, in a weak effort to haul her back.

"Neither do I," agreed Greg. "He probably has another girlfriend at university."

"I'll be fifteen by the time Led Zeppelin arrive," I said.

I was pleased at that. Like all fourteen-year-olds, I couldn't wait to be older.

The air was rich with the aroma of incense. After picking up the habit from Zed I never lost it. I still like the fragrance. It gives me the feeling that I've been to India without actually having to travel.

fourteen

LATER IN THE EVENING, I stood with Greg under a pale street light, smoking cigarettes and talking about Led Zeppelin and dragons. In our imaginations, Greg and I were joint masters of the Fabulous Dragon Army of Gothar, which stood alone against the Monstrous Hordes of Xotha. The Monstrous Hordes of Xotha were led by Kuthimas, a mad sorcerer of enormous power whose only ambition was to take over the world. He already ruled most of it. The only areas which remained free were Glasgow and the hidden realm of Atlantis. Without the stern resistance of Greg, myself, and the Fabulous Dragon Army of Gothar, our planet would already have been doomed. We spent a lot of time in this imaginary world. It was better than school.

We stared out at the dark skies. There was a chill in the air. Just the sort of chill that might precede an attack by Kuthimas and the orcish forces. They had dragons as well, and they were bigger than ours, with more powerful fire. Only the fact that Greg and I were such skilful dragon riders enabled us to keep winning battles. It was always close. We could never relax our vigil.

"It would be easier if Atlantis was to rise from beneath the sea," said Greg, and I nodded in agreement. The underwater survivors of Atlantis were our allies but there weren't many of them and it took them a long time to fly to Glasgow.

Unusually, Cherry appeared. She was walking home after a violin lesson, carrying the instrument in a battered black case. Though it was late in the evening, she was still wearing her school blazer. No one else, not even the dumbest kid on their first day at school, would wear their uniform when they didn't have to. We groaned loudly, so she could hear.

"Can I play?" she asked.

I was outraged that anyone might think that I was playing. I was fourteen years old. I didn't play any more.

"Go away and write your diary," I said.

"I want to be in the Dragon Army," pleaded Cherry.

Greg and I exchanged pained frowns. We weren't certain exactly how Cherry had learned of the Dragon Army. We presumed she had been spying on us. Certainly we had never mentioned our extended dragon fantasy to Suzy, or anyone else. If Cherry were to make it public it would be extremely damaging. People would mock.

"Go away," said Greg.

"I want to play," said Cherry.

The streetlights were reflected in her glasses.

"Go away you stupid freckled freak," I told her. "Can't you see we're busy?"

Cherry turned sharply and hurried away. I was pleased. A harsh mention of her freckles was usually enough to get rid of her. It was a sensitive subject.

Later that night we added Cherry to the list of our enemies who were in the Monstrous Hordes of Xotha. She became the bastard daughter of Kuthimas, an evil princess in her own right who led a troop of hideous red dragons. We shot her down in flames and she perished in quite an unpleasant manner, crushed under her dragon.

Most of our enemies ended up this way. The gym teacher at school was forever being burned by dragon fire and Bassy, a large schoolmate who bullied us, met a grisly end on a regular basis.

Later on, I was worried in case Cherry told Suzy about the Dragon Army. I knew that Suzy would think it was foolish and infantile. Suzy might be fabulous, beautiful and alluring, but she just wasn't the sort of person to ever imagine she was soaring over Glasgow on a dragon, fighting off the orcish hordes.

fifteen

IT WAS INTRIGUING THAT SUZY HAD BLONDE HAIR. Perhaps she was of Viking descent. Maybe her ancestors had arrived in a longboat to do some pillaging, and decided to stay. Led Zeppelin had a song about this, 'Immigrant Song', where Vikings from the land of ice and snow are on their way to ravage their neighbours.

Some years later it was also intriguing to me that the woman in the Nefertiti hat had blonde hair. Her hair was not naturally blonde, it was dyed, and contrasted strongly with her dark skin. I liked the way it looked.

In Glasgow in the early seventies, no one dyed their hair. It hadn't been invented yet. Painful sexual desire, on the other hand, had now been discovered, and I was an early casualty.

It was made worse by Suzy confessing her dissatisfaction with Zed. Whenever I met Suzy on the way to school, she would tell me what a useless boyfriend Zed was. He was always going out with friends and leaving her behind or else getting drunk and disgracing himself. Her parents had started to disapprove of the relationship. They had never particularly liked Zed. Although he was never uncivil to them, they regarded him as far too weird-looking, and almost certainly a bad influence on their daughter. When tales of his misbehaviour at school and other places filtered back to them they began to dislike him more and more.

Suzy found herself in the uncomfortable position of defending Zed to her parents while being annoyed at him herself. She was confused and unhappy as she described her situation to me.

Although I had no idea what advice to give to any girl who was having problems with her boyfriend, I knew instinctively that it was a good thing to listen. To listen for a long time, if necessary. I didn't interrupt with my own dreams or problems. I didn't dismiss Suzy's cares with a hearty, 'don't worry about it, it will work out fine in the end'. I just listened, and I could see that this went down well with Suzy.

This was a valuable lesson for the future. I developed into a great listener to women's problems. I have a talent for it. Women who are depressed or anxious can talk to me for hours.

"That is because you want to sleep with those troubled women," says Manx, who remembers that we first went to bed together after she spent a whole Saturday night telling me how unhappy she was about everything. I maintain that she was much less unhappy the next day, but Manx still claims things were only ten per cent better if that, and it faded by lunch-time.

Anyway, that was all some years ago. Now Manx and I are just friends, so she feels free to strongly criticise my every action.

"Well all right Manx, I have often benefited from the depression of my female friends. But I don't think that's so bad. After all, it's surely better to sleep with someone who is at least prepared to listen to your problems for hours. Whether I really care or not probably doesn't matter. I'm still providing a good service."

Manx laughs. Some years ago, she wouldn't have laughed, she would have given me a stern lecture about exploitation of woman. In those days we were both more sincere about the things we believed in, and we liked ourselves better.

Back when I was fifteen, listening to Suzy's troubles, I was painfully sincere. I cared about her distress. So did Greg. Every day we would sit in his room, listening to Led Zeppelin and discussing Suzy.

"You think maybe Zed gets too drunk to do it?" wondered Greg.

I shrugged. I didn't know how drunk anyone would have to be before they were unable to do it.

"I wish Suzy would sleep with me," said Greg. "I reckon it's only a matter of time. She's taking the pill. She must be keen on sex. And if Zed's too drunk to perform what better replacement than me?"

Greg lit some incense and put *Led Zeppelin Four* on the turntable. We sang the guitar riffs, and shook our hair, and wondered how we might succeed in making Suzy sweat and groove like the women did in the songs. The way Robert Plant sung, it sounded easy enough, but we were both aware that we were not Robert Plant.

Greg positioned the empty album cover carefully on the shelf where it would not be stepped on or have tea spilled on it. He was always very careful with his records. I never was. My record collection was a shambles. These days it's worse. My CDs are strewn all over the place and many of the cases are cracked where I've stood on them. I've never been the sort of person who looks after their records well, or catalogues all their music with loving care. After all, they're only plastic discs. If one gets damaged you can always buy another one. To hell with them, I say.

I've always suspected that people who worry about record care, cataloguing and formats all the time don't actually care for the music very much.

Greg peered through the curtains at the dark clouds above. He wondered if we might be due an attack from Kuthimas the Slayer and his Monstrous Dragon Hordes. It seemed likely. Lately he had been very quiet. We suspected he was building up his reserves.

"We should send a message to Atlantis," said Greg. "Make sure they're ready."

Greg's hair was a few inches longer than mine. He was two inches taller than me. He had slightly better clothes and was a little better looking. He was more confident and got on with other people better than I did. I was quite aware of all this but it was all right, he wasn't so far ahead in any of these departments as to make our friendship impossible. But as we looked out of the window, scanning the skies for a possible attack by the Monstrous Hordes of Xotha, it did strike me for the first time that if Suzy were to ditch Zed, and start looking around for a new boyfriend, she was more likely to choose Greg than me.

sixteen

NEFERTITI WAS QUEEN OF EGYPT IN 1353 BC. She was the wife of Pharaoh Akhenaton, who shocked the priesthood by radically reforming the state religion. As well as being a prominent political figure, she was a famous beauty. Two of her daughters also went on to be Egyptian queens.

The famous sculpture of Nefertiti was found in Tel el-Amarna and now resides in the Egyptian museum in Berlin. I have a little model of it on my mantelpiece. It's a beautiful sculpture.

Every time I looked at my small statue of Nefertiti, it reminded me of the woman wearing that hat in Brixton Road. I wondered if I would ever meet her. I hoped so. She had to be an interesting person to be wearing a hat like that, and have such brightly dyed hair.

I finally met her at a party. I didn't know whose party it was, I had just gone along with some friends. There was a small patch of waste ground at the back of the house which might have been a garden if there had been any grass or flowers. The people who lived there had set up some bricks and lit a fire. Smoke and sparks flew in the wind, choking anyone who ventured too close.

Standing just far back enough from the fire to avoid the smoke was the woman in the Nefertiti hat, still wearing the hat. I wanted to talk to her but I couldn't think of anything to say, except to compliment her on her fine headgear. That would just have to do.

"What a fabulous hat. It's the best hat in the world and you look just like Nefertiti. I expect everyone says that to you all the time."

"No," she replied. "Some people have never heard of Nefertiti, and I think most people are too embarrassed to come right out with a compliment anyway."

She was pleased at the compliment. I gave her a beer which I was carrying in a plastic Tesco bag and we had an interesting talk about ancient Egypt. For the only time in my life I was grateful that our teachers had made us do all those projects.

She told me her name was Manx. Then two of her friends came up and told her it was time to go.

"I have to catch a plane in the morning," she said. "I'm going to Thailand. I'll be back in a year or so."

It was some time till I saw Manx again, but I was pleased I had introduced myself.

seventeen

THERE ARE VARIOUS REASONS behind Manx's current depression, one of these reasons being that Manx has always been depressed.

"I was very depressed at school," she said to me once, when I was describing an incident from my own school days, and I listened politely.

These days there are other things to get her down. She's sad that the relationship with her child's father didn't work out. She's depressed about how hard it is bringing up a baby on her own. She never has enough money and she never gets enough sleep. Manx was never the sort of person who enjoyed rising before midday but these days she is up at dawn, trying to make progress with her studies before Malachi wakes and demands feeding.

Her social life has greatly diminished. Most of her friends can't wait around for ever while Manx finds a baby-sitter. They don't want to wait till next week before going out, they want to go out now.

"They don't visit much any more. I know why. It's because I'm such a boring baby person. They've been going to the pictures or fucking someone they met at a nightclub or making websites for their businesses, and all I've been doing is shopping for nappies. How dull is that? If I was one of my friends I wouldn't visit me either. I'm too tedious."

I'm surprised at all this. I had an idea that having a baby filled the mother up with happy chemicals which kept her going for a year or two, even in difficult circumstances. Manx says that if these happy chemicals ever existed in her body, they made a very quick departure.

"And they were pretty weak chemicals anyway, not to be compared with the effects of the mind-altering substances I used to rely on. Which, of course, I am not allowed to take any more because I'm breast-feeding. Nowadays I don't even take aspirin, and that is annoying because not getting enough sleep is giving me a terrible fucking headache."

I don't mean to give the impression that Manx does not love her baby. She does. It is just her life she hates.

Manx tells me that she particularly dislikes getting old.

"My life is finished. I'll never see another band or dance in a club. And I'll never be able to travel to Thailand and India and Australia again."

Manx also suffers from the very common problem of punishing herself for her own depression. She feels guilty about it.

"The fact that I can't travel or go to see bands any more shouldn't depress me. I must be a really shallow person."

I try and reassure Manx that she isn't shallow. Manx won't be reassured.

"I'm fat and out of condition. I look terrible. Even if I could go out I wouldn't. What's the point of going out anywhere when you look like this?"

I'm worried. I see that Manx is plunging down the precipice and is in need of help. Soon after having her baby, Manx signed up to do a course in computer animation at a local college. She goes there twice a week and brings projects home to work at on her computer. I thought this was a good idea, and still do, but it has caused Manx great stress.

"Why did I want to learn about computer animation? Or anything? It was foolish."

"You wanted your life to keep moving forward in a strong positive manner."

Manx states that if she ever said such a thing, she must have been suffering from some strong postnatal delusions at the time.

"I think the problem is that you never wear the Nefertiti hat any more," I tell her.

She looks at me like I'm a mad person.

"The Nefertiti hat? I haven't worn that for years. How could I wear it? You expect me to push a pushchair wearing my Nefertiti hat? In my condition? Looking like this? People would mock me."

Manx is adamant so I let it drop, but I don't forget about it. I am convinced she would feel a lot better about everything if she would wear her Nefertiti hat again. It has to be a cheerful thing to do.

I've made us a pot of tea. Malachi the baby is slumbering on the couch, looking cute. Manx looks at the box of books which I have now brought into the front room.

"Aren't you going to open it?"

"I can't face it yet. I wish I hadn't agreed to judge this competition."

"Tell them you've changed your mind."

"I can't. I've already spent the cheque."

Manx glances in my mirror. She is pleased at the results of her Masquisuperbe All Over Face Glow. Pleased enough to have bought some cheek and lip stain from Benefit, to give her some afterglow.

I compliment her on it. "It's great afterglow."

"It won't last. I'm worn out. By tomorrow the afterglow will have disappeared for ever."

eighteen

"TELL ME MORE ABOUT LED ZEPPELIN AND SUZY," says Manx, so I do.

Led Zeppelin Four was released towards the end of 1971 and the band spent the next year on tour. I'd read about their progress around the globe in the music papers. Already in 1972 they had played in America, Canada, Japan, Australia and New Zealand.

I sat and day-dreamed of Led Zeppelin leaving Valhalla in their mighty cosmic Zeppelin and flying down to Japan to step on stage like the majestic warriors they were. It was easy in those days to dream about things like that. So when the Zeppelins start flying out of Valhalla, as they do later on in this book, it is because as a young teenager that's how I thought about music.

At the start of the seventies, bands would often sing about cosmic warriors. Led Zeppelin were never actually into space imagery, being more given to Tolkienesque themes of elves and dragons, in between a lot of white man's blues. Much of their lyrics were about having difficult times with women.

These were all things I could relate to. I spent my spare time pretending to be a master of dragons, and if I ever had a relationship with a woman, I expected it would give me problems.

Led Zeppelin were never going to be the sort of band who sang protest songs. And that, I still feel strongly, was something in their favour.

As for Zed, his fanaticism about Led Zeppelin was as intense as a relationship could be between a boy and his band. His walls were covered with posters and he could quote reams of their lyrics. He had tapes of their radio sessions which included songs that were not released till twenty years afterwards. He had a bootleg album of a concert in Japan and bought an embroidered waistcoat the same as Robert Plant was wearing in a picture in the *NME*. Sometimes it seemed to me that when Zed finished school he would join the band, just be inducted in by some natural process.

I first saw Zed drunk when he was thirteen. I was eleven. He arrived at my door when my parents were out and went to sleep in my bed till he had sobered up enough to walk the short distance home. When I told Greg about this he was jealous, jealous that I had been able to do a favour for someone as cool as Zed.

Zed had a very small spoon on a chain which he told us was a coke spoon, something we had heard about from America. I doubt very much if there was any cocaine around in Glasgow at the time, and if there was it certainly hadn't reached our school, but owning the coke spoon was yet another important thing in Zed's favour. It made him seem like a man who had been around. Like a man who could walk right up to Led Zeppelin and talk about things they'd be interested in.

I knew they wouldn't be interested in my Dragon Army. If we ever met, I'd keep that quiet.

nineteen

I WAS FOURTEEN when Zed began going out with Suzy. I was distressed when it happened. So was Greg, though neither of us were surprised. Listening to Led Zeppelin, we had already realised that life with regard to women was never going to be easy. I was certain that I would never have a girlfriend. Greg was less pessimistic.

"It'll be better in a year or two," he said.

We discussed it while sitting in a cafe, drinking tea and smoking. Almost all of the other fourteen-year-olds we knew smoked cigarettes.

"I knew he liked her."

"So did I."

Last year, worried by the possibility, I'd asked Zed what he thought about Suzy. He had shrugged. I understood that. It was always safer to wait for some positive signs from the other person before admitting your own interest. I don't know what positive signs Suzy gave to Zed; they happened when I wasn't around. Anyway, they were now going out together and that was that. Greg and I were depressed but there was nothing to be done about it, except sit around and complain.

Although Greg was my best friend, I was pleased that I had been with Zed, rather than Greg, when I first heard the name 'Led Zeppelin'. I think I was twelve. School was closed due to a heavy fall of snow which had caused a power cut. We were sitting on a bench in front of a row of shops, doing nothing. Some younger kids were throwing snowballs at each other. I was hoping no one threw one at me. I didn't want to look stupid in front of Zed.

Jim appeared, a person I only knew by sight. He was a couple of years older than Zed and without doubt the coolest person in school, the first to wear an afghan coat. Jim was drinking a can of McEwan's Export.

"What's your favourite band?" he asked.

I looked blank. I knew that any answer I came out with would be wrong. Too poppy probably, which would get me laughed at. Zed answered confidently.

"Steppenwolf," he said.

That was a good answer. Steppenwolf were thoroughly credible. Not poppy at all. Jim nodded in a thoughtful manner which showed that while not exactly impressed, neither was he appalled.

"Not bad," he said. "Though they sound like Led Zeppelin tuning up."

After Jim had gone I asked Zed who Led Zeppelin were. He was surprised at my ignorance. Apparently they had a record out already.

"I'll play you them," he said.

It was cold, and starting to snow again. I thought about the band as I walked home. Led Zeppelin. It was a good name. I liked them already.

It was after this incident that Zed became such a Led Zeppelin fanatic. Possibly Zed was influenced by Jim in the same way that I was influenced by Zed. After Jim left school to be a painter and decorator, Zed took over his position as coolest person around.

I don't think I ever affected anyone like that. Neither did Greg. No one ever developed a favourite band because we recommended them.

twenty

GREG CALLED FOR ME and we went round to Suzy's house. Suzy was in a cheerful mood because she'd been out with Zed the night before and he hadn't been three hours late or turned up smelling of beer or committed any other outrage.

Greg and I were secretly disappointed. We liked it that Zed was always committing outrages. It made him more of a hero for us. He was the only rebel we knew.

I don't remember ever wondering why Zed was like this. Zed's father was a very authoritarian character who worked as a civilian administrator for the police, so perhaps it wouldn't have required much analysis to find the roots of Zed's rebellion. But if I was aware of that at the time, it was only very dimly. Zed committing outrages just seemed to be the natural order of things, and not to require analysis.

Zed and Suzy loved each other more than they admitted. They were one of those couples with a powerful bond that even the worst of circumstances could not entirely break. Even when they came to dislike each other, which they did, they couldn't manage to fall out of love.

There was a school bag on Suzy's bedroom floor. It stood out as an unusual item because Suzy never would have carried such a dull thing. She had a hippy patchwork bag that she brought to school, and a smart leather bag for any occasions that required dressing up.

"Cherry left it here."

"You let her visit you?" said Greg, feigning amazement.

Suzy smiled.

"She's not so bad. Apart from those glasses."

We laughed.

When Suzy's mother called her away to answer a phone call, Greg and I leapt for the bag and started rummaging around inside. It had struck us both at the same time that if we could locate something incriminating, we could blackmail Cherry with it and prevent her from ever blabbing about the Fabulous Dragon Army.

Thoughts often used to strike Greg and me at the same time. It was because we had been fighting in the same army for so long. We always knew what to expect.

"The diary!" hissed Greg, and stuffed it inside his coat seconds before Suzy returned.

"Zed's coming over," she told us.

We were all happy about this.

Suzy put on the first Led Zeppelin album. She wanted to be certain that Led Zeppelin were playing when Zed arrived. Otherwise, he might be disappointed.

Suzy kicked Cherry's bag under the bed, out of the way. Zed and I giggled, because we had the diary.

Suzy had a music paper and we read about a fight in London between skinheads and some hippy squatters. We had skinheads in Glasgow, skinheads at our school. This year they'd grown their hair another few millimetres, and they wore long black coats and white trousers, turned up high over their boots. They were scary, and we avoided them.

Suzy spent a while looking lovingly at a picture of Marc Bolan. This was dull to Greg and me. We wanted her to turn the page but we didn't say anything. In her happy state, Suzy was looking beautiful and we could put up with her staring at a picture of Marc Bolan.

Zed arrived and he was pleased to see us all. He was funny and entertaining and he showed us an underground comic he'd got from some students in town. It was a good night, but walking home I was unhappy. It was clear that Zed deserved Suzy more than me, but no amount of rationalisation could make me like it. My love for Suzy was becoming a dragon which was starting to chew up my belly. I couldn't bear the feeling but there was nothing to do about it

Sometimes it seemed like too much to cope with. The only relief I got was in listening to Led Zeppelin. They had suffered too. I could hear it in their songs.

We got three days off school when the power workers went on strike. In 1972 there were a lot of strikes. Power workers, miners, dockers, car workers, even teachers. I was fully in support of this. Anything that got us time off school was a cause worth supporting.

twenty-one

THE DIARY WAS A DISASTROUS EPISODE. Greg took it home with him to read and the next morning he phoned me before I left for school, something he would only do under the most urgent circumstances.

"You won't believe what's in Cherry's diary."

He was obviously bursting with excitement. I skipped breakfast and hurried out to meet him. When I reached his house, Greg was outside waiting for me, the diary in his hand.

"Cherry's a poet," he said.

"You mean there's poems in her diary?"

Greg nodded. I could see why he'd been excited. Any poetry written by Cherry was bound to be worth reading. Just to know that she wrote poems was amusing in itself. I grabbed the book.

"'A Poem to my Mythical Older Brother'."

"What sort of pathetic title is that?"

I read quickly through it. It was fairly obscure and I couldn't say if it was any good or not, but it implied quite strongly that Cherry spent time talking to an imaginary older brother, so it was certainly funny.

"'A Poem About Having Nowhere to Go After Midnight'."

"She should get some friends," said Greg, and started reading it out loud.

"Look, she's in love."

I was startled at the thought of Cherry being in love with anyone.

"Who with?"

It didn't say. The poem was dedicated to a mysterious object of passion and entitled 'My Love for Z'.

This was very funny. The thought of dumb little Cherry in love had us clutching at lamp-posts for support.

There was a lot of verse in the diary. It also recorded her daily activities, like going to violin lessons and shopping with her mother – she seemed to enjoy shopping with her mother – but every few pages there would be another poem, always with some sad title like 'The Loneliness of the Moon', or 'The Abandoned Dog Howls in Pain'.

Greg was hugely entertained, and so was I. We stood turning the pages, reading Cherry's neat handwriting in which she gave details of her music lessons, her shopping trips, and her unrequited passion. When Greg's mother came out of the house on her way to work, we quickly hid the diary and started off to school, reading as we walked. There seemed to be a lot about Z.

We looked again at the poem 'My Love for Z'.

"Maybe she's in love with Zed?"

"Wait till Suzy hears," said Greg, and we laughed at the thought of how Suzy would react to Cherry lusting after her boyfriend.

The whole thing seemed so ludicrous that by the time we reached school my ribs ached from laughing. The thought of Cherry, with her mass of unruly red hair, freckles and terrible glasses, feeling passion for anyone, was the most hilarious thing we could imagine.

We had some idea of keeping the diary secret but this didn't last for long. In the class where we had to gather for roll call every morning, I leant over and whispered to Suzy about Cherry being in love with Zed and writing poems about wishing for a mythical older brother. Suzy started laughing and then she had to tell the person next to her what she was laughing about. Soon everyone knew that Cherry, the odd looking kid from the year below us, had been writing poems and falling in love. Everyone agreed that this was a very funny thing.

Greg did a good impersonation of Cherry sawing away at her violin, and saying things like 'I'm so unhappy, nobody likes me,' and everybody laughed.

Suzy whispered to us that it was mean to have stolen the diary, but she was soon reading out loud some of the more embarrassing lines from Cherry's youthful poems.

The whole class was mocking Cherry, but it all went wrong when Bassy grabbed the diary off the girl next to Suzy and started to read. He flicked over a few pages and then howled.

"She says she wants to join the Dragon Army of Gothar. What's that?"

Bassy looked at us. I looked at Greg. Greg frowned. I frowned. It seemed that Cherry had recorded details of our dragon-flying exploits. In quite a lot of detail, from the extract which Bassy read out to everyone.

"They are in contact with the hidden realm of Atlantis," quoted Bassy, and everyone roared with laughter.

The object of mockery ceased to be Cherry. It was now me and Greg. I made a grab for the diary but Bassy brushed me off and then the teacher came in. At the end of the class, Bassy kept the diary.

Greg and I realised that we had made a bad mistake. We should have fully examined the document before subjecting it to public ridicule. Now we were being ridiculed as well.

"The stupid little bitch," spat Greg. "What did she have to write about that for?"

We hated Cherry for getting us into trouble. Now we would be forever humiliated as the boys who, at the age of fifteen, still pretended they flew about on dragons, talked to Atlanteans, and rescued princesses.

twenty-two

IT WAS A BAD DAY AT SCHOOL. The French teacher laughed at my accent as I failed to get my Glaswegian tongue round some simple French nouns. The Deputy Headmaster stopped Greg and me in the corridor and started harassing us to get our hair cut. He went on about it for a long time. It seemed as if the entire reputation of the school depended on us having short hair. Possibly even the entire reputation of Scotland.

Bassy was tireless in his mockery of our fantasy world. We already hated Bassy. He played football and he didn't like Led Zeppelin. He pushed us around and there wasn't anything we could do about it.

Worst of all, Cherry actually marched up to us at lunch-time and demanded her diary back.

This drew a large and interested crowd. Word of Cherry's hopeless passion and poetry had now spread and Cherry herself had been the subject of much scorn. As she approached, she looked like she was about to launch into a long speech, but instead she just asked for the diary back and then burst into tears.

I didn't know what to say. Everything had gone disastrously wrong. I had to admit that I didn't have the diary any more. Bassy wouldn't give it back. Cherry went away crying. Public opinion turned against Greg and me. Everyone had been entertained by Cherry's private thoughts but as she went sobbing across the playground, friendless, powerless, tears pouring out from under her thick glasses, clutching her tattered black violin case, everyone now decided that it had been a terrible thing to do, to steal her diary.

"It's a shame," said Suzy, even though she'd enjoyed it as well. She said she would never speak to us again unless Cherry got her diary back, and neither would her friends.

"It's the sort of behaviour you'd expect from someone who pretends he flies around on a dragon," said one of Suzy's pretty companions. "You should grow up."

Only Bassy and his friends felt no sympathy and continued to go around reading out Cherry's diary to anyone who would listen. It seemed like things would never end till Zed, who had missed school in the morning, turned up in the afternoon. When he heard what had been happening he went to Bassy and told him to hand the diary over. Bassy was larger and stronger than Zed but was unable to resist Zed's moral authority. Bassy meekly handed it over, all the while laughing about what a pair of homos Greg and I were, and what a freak Cherry was.

Zed returned the diary to Cherry. She emerged from her shell just enough to thank him, then lapsed back into her irredeemable misery.

"It wasn't a very nice thing to do," said Zed to Greg and me, but he didn't lecture us about it.

twenty-three

CHERRY'S DIARY was not the only bad thing that happened around then. Life was becoming more difficult by the minute. So far I'd been able to submerge my sexual frustration in the Fabulous Dragon Army but this no longer seemed enough. I'd go to sleep thinking about Suzy and wake up even more obsessed.

To make matters worse, it appeared that I might be frustrated for the rest of my life because Greg told me that a girl in our class had called me fat. This took me by surprise. I hadn't even considered this possibility. I'd never thought about the shape of my body before.

I looked at myself in the mirror. It seemed to me that I might be a little overweight. That was bad. It occurred to me that if I looked overweight even to myself, it must be much worse for everyone else. To other people I might look as big as a house. They would hate me, and they would have good reason to.

My life was heading for disaster. If I carried on being a fat person no woman would ever want to go out with me. No woman would even want to be seen with me. I would never be successful at anything and I wouldn't have any friends. I wouldn't deserve them, being so obese.

I looked at my posters of Led Zeppelin and realised how slender they were. They were much thinner than me. It seemed incredible that I'd never noticed this before. Had I actually considered going to see this band whilst being overweight? What a stupid notion. Quite probably, overweight people weren't allowed in to see Led Zeppelin.

So I stopped eating, and became thin. From that day, I have had a very uncomfortable relationship with food. I am never happy eating. I don't much like food and I don't trust it. I can't do anything spontaneous when it comes to food. There is no way, for instance, that I could go with friends on the spur of the moment to a restaurant. Who knows what damaging ingredients there might be in the strange and unfamiliar meal.

I went off the whole idea of food. I didn't like to think of it inside me. I became a vegetarian just so I had less food to think about. Eating has caused me all sorts of problems in my life, problems which have veered, at times, towards mental illness.

However, on the positive side, I have always remained thin.

twenty-four

AFTER ZED PLAYED ME THE RECORDS, it didn't take me long to become obsessed with Led Zeppelin. It was a better sound than anything else. I bought the first two albums and spent a long time looking at the covers. *Led Zeppelin One* was quite exciting with its black and white Zeppelin going down in flames, but the cover of *Led Zeppelin Two* was a wonderland. There was a really mighty Zeppelin flying overhead and under this the band posed with a group of German airmen. It looked as though the band was part of the squadron.

Searchlights played among marble columns, giving the whole picture an air of grandeur and magnificence. I loved that record cover.

When we finally got a record player, which was around the time that *Led Zeppelin Three* appeared, I used to sit in my bedroom and listen to them over and over again. I listened to the records all the time, before and after school and all day at the weekends. Everything seemed better. I stopped regarding myself as a kid. I was now a man with three Led Zeppelin albums. No one could argue with that.

Greg was similarly affected. He listened to Led Zeppelin all the time too. The music erected some sort of protective barrier between us and the rest of the world. Whenever anything went wrong or felt bad, there was always a Led Zeppelin album to retreat to.

Our favourite track was 'Whole Lotta Love', a seething storm of guitars, sex and psychedelia. I wonder how many times I have listened to that over the years. Thousands of times. Millions of times. Da-da da-da DA da-da da-da.

We heard that Cherry was planning to go to the Led Zeppelin gig. That was annoying. At least Phil wasn't. Phil liked classical music, and played violin with Cherry. Sometimes they would visit each other's houses, just to play music together. Greg and I were baffled by this. We could only presume that their parents made them do it. Sometimes we'd hear the faint sound of violins coming from Cherry's open window, but we could make nothing of the music. It just seemed to go on and on for no reason. There was never a good riff to get hold of.

We never spoke to Phil. On the very rare occasions he appeared on the street he was careful never to make eye contact with anyone, even though he had known us at primary school. There, he was always top of the class.

The teacher used to bring in special advanced books for him and he'd study on his own, never appearing in the playground. If he had, he'd just have been mocked. The only time we ever saw him those days was when he was walking along the street with his violin on his way to Cherry's, or being driven by his parents to the school for exceptional children.

On a particularly freezing night, I was hanging around with Greg on the tiny patch of scrubby grass at the end of the road. We were watching the cars pull up at Phil's house. Four or five cars, which seemed like a large social gathering. Men in suits and women in smart dresses hurried indoors from the cold. Phil's parents were having some sort of party.

We huddled against the wooden fence, drawing our coats tight against the weather, humming Led Zeppelin tunes and scanning the skies. Unexpectedly, Phil appeared in the street. Even more surprisingly, when he saw us he headed in our direction. He stumbled, picked himself up, and when he reached us he sat down heavily on the grass. He didn't say anything, just sat beside us looking at the ground, and mumbling.

I was perplexed until Greg laughed and said, "He's drunk."

And so it turned out to be. Phil had surreptitiously drunk some wine at his parents' gathering and it was having a powerful effect. He leaned over and threw up quite violently, many times, retching and retching till there was nothing more to come up.

Greg and I couldn't help feeling sympathetic. You had to admire anyone who sneaked some alcohol from their parents then stumbled outside to be sick.

"I'm so unhappy," said Phil, and retched again.

Greg and I looked at each other. We were puzzled again. Why would Phil tell us he was unhappy?

"I'm in love with Cherry," he said.

I had an overwhelming urge to laugh. Only the sight of Phil, retching pathetically, prevented me. Phil, still strongly under the effect of the wine, carried on like this for some time. He was very miserable. He was in love with Cherry, but he knew she was in love with someone else and it was tormenting him. The idea that a fat clever person like Phil could be tormented by love was news to us, and took some digesting. It was all so extraordinary and tragic that we didn't even ridicule the man for being in love with such a fool as Cherry.

"But she doesn't even notice me because we're friends," said Phil, and started crying. "And she's in love with someone else."

Phil shook his head hopelessly, then he was sick again, and lay down on the frozen grass.

twenty-five

AT THE SAME TIME as I was judging the literary competition, I was trying to write a cartoon for television. The cartoon grew out of a comic I'd written a few years previously, 'The Fluffy Avenger and her Amazing Powers of Poetic Justice.'

The Fluffy Avenger gained her miraculous powers for doing good when she was struck by a comet that had passed through the aura of a Buddha while he was ascending towards Nirvana. She went round punishing wrongdoers in whatever manner seemed most appropriate to her, and while this wasn't actually all that original an idea, I was fond of the character. So fond of her, in fact, that she became an imaginary friend, and remains so today, along with Socrates, the fairies, and various others.

"Fluffy Avenger, the government is knocking down a forest to build a new motorway! What are you going to do about it?"

"I'll turn the bulldozers into giant bouncy castles for children to play on, and plant a huge oak tree right in the middle of the Transport Minister's bedroom."

"Great idea, Fluffy Avenger! It's funny and it's appropriate."

You can't argue with that.

I didn't have imaginary friends when I was very young. I developed them as I got older. I have quite an extensive fantasy sex life as well. Often while I'm strolling down the street, I'm wrapped up in the most surprising activities. I expect a lot of people are.

Manx tells me that, as result of having a baby, she is now too tired to have any sort of sex life, real or imagined. In an attempt to bring some joy into her life, I've brought her a Kemistry and Storm CD as a present. Kemistry and Storm are two female DJs who mix drum and bass tracks till it sounds like there are dragons fighting overhead. I'm hoping that the incredible noise might shock Manx back into life. Manx likes the CD but it depresses her in a way I had not anticipated. Kemistry's skin is the same light brown shade as Manx's and what's more she has bleached blonde hair. This reminds Manx of the way she used to look, which makes her miserable.

"I wish I was a drum and bass DJ instead of being overweight and stuck in the house," she says. "I'll never be able to dye my hair blonde again."

"If you were to wear the Nefertiti hat your hair wouldn't matter," I suggest, cunningly.

"I'm not wearing that hat," says Manx, firmly.

I change the subject.

"I have big news. I opened the box of books."

"How do they look?" asks Manx.

I admit I haven't actually taken them out of the box yet.

"But I'll get round to it soon."

Baby Malachi starts crying. Manx gets in a worse mood. She is behind with some piece of computer animation and if she doesn't get a good mark she might fail this part of the course.

Like me, Manx has always been dissatisfied with life. She stares glumly at the cover of the CD.

"I wish it was Kemistry, Storm and Manx."

On the way home, I give money to the beggar who always sits near to the Kentucky Fried Chicken. It might never have occurred to me to give money to beggars if it hadn't been for Zed. Once in St George's Square in the centre of Glasgow, I saw Zed with some friends, older youths I didn't know. I was hanging back, not wanting to embarrass Zed in front of his friends by saying hello. As I watched, he handed some coins to a tramp.

Zed's friends were mockingly amused by this. They thought it was a silly thing to do. It wasn't something I would have thought of doing myself. Zed was unconcerned. No such mockery could affect him.

Thinking about Zed now, it doesn't bother me at all that I hero-worshipped him. He was generous, and he was funny, and those are good things to be. I think about him when I give money to beggars.

twenty-six

AFTER THE INCIDENT OF THE DIARY, Cherry no longer watched us as we stood under the street light. We were pleased at this, but very unhappy because Suzy was annoyed.

"You broke her heart," said Suzy.

We didn't care that we'd broken Cherry's heart but we couldn't stand Suzy being angry with us. Greg and I were at a loss. We couldn't understand why Suzy was now angry about us being mean to Cherry. She didn't even particularly like Cherry. She only tolerated her because their parents were friendly.

"It's us that are suffering," I said to Greg, morosely. That day, as usual, Bassy had ridiculed us about the Fabulous Dragon Army. He flapped his arms, pretending to fly. His friends joined in, and when we tried to walk on they stood right in front of us so we couldn't get past.

"Just ignore them," advised Zed later, joining us under the lamp-post. He was carrying three Led Zeppelin albums under his arm. Zed had a dark blue T-shirt with Indian style embroidery in golden thread around the neck. Greg and I were jealous. It made us dissatisfied with our own plain T-shirts.

He told us that Suzy said we had to apologise to Cherry. This seemed very unreasonable. Zed said that he couldn't get Suzy to change her mind and anyway, didn't we owe Cherry an apology?

We rebelled against this but Zed reminded us that Cherry had asked Suzy to get her a ticket for Led Zeppelin so, if we didn't make up, we wouldn't even be able to go with Suzy to the gig. It was all becoming too much for us, so we trooped off to say we were sorry.

This was one of the most humiliating experiences of my youth. Almost as bad as the time that Suzy persuaded me that Carol from up the hill was attracted to me and I should ask her out. When I did, Carol looked at me in blank amazement before hurrying off to tell her friends the bizarre news.

There was a small garden in front of Cherry's house with a neat lawn and a few small bushes. We traipsed up the concrete path and knocked at the door.

"I'm sorry we stole your diary," I said.

"So am I," said Greg.

"Okay," said Cherry.

There was a long silence, then Cherry asked us if we would like to come inside. My skin was crawling with the embarrassment of all this. We declined the invitation and Cherry looked disappointed. We escaped as quickly as we could and headed for Suzy's house.

"We apologised to Cherry."

Suzy smiled. We were back in favour. It was a relief. Being sexually fixated on a girl who wouldn't even speak to me had been hard to take.

Suzy was wearing a new T-shirt with a picture of Robert Plant on it, a present from Zed. Her hair was fluffy blonde and she looked fabulous. We told her about Phil getting drunk and confessing his hopeless love for Cherry. We were expecting Suzy to laugh but, again confounding our expectations, she found it sad.

"It's romantic," she said. "Hopeless love always is."

I wondered if she would find my hopeless love for her romantic. Maybe. Maybe not. I wasn't going to risk a confession.

"Should we tell Cherry about it?"

Suzy said that we shouldn't. Not yet anyway.

"Give Phil more time to work up his courage."

As we were now back in favour with Suzy, the

Dragon Army was in good form. We had recently suffered some serious defeats. Morale had been low. Now, bolstered by Suzy's smile, we were able to chase the Monstrous Hordes of Xotha from the skies. Glasgow was once more safe for humanity.

It was almost time to go and queue for Led Zeppelin tickets. Even the thought of queuing for a ticket to see the band had Greg and me shaking with excitement.

"Look," I said, holding up my hand, "I'm shaking with excitement."

twenty-seven

I WAS SITTING IN THE PARK with Greg, talking about the forthcoming gig. Zed appeared, his afghan coat flapping in the chilling wind. Zed was now seventeen and his drinking had increased. He often showed up drunk in the evenings. I had never been drunk. Greg might have been.

"You're not wearing my T-shirt," said Zed, which I didn't understand till later when Greg told me that Zed had given him his blue embroidered shirt, the one I so admired. He was going to wear it at the concert. I was surprised at this, and jealous. I still only had a plain T-shirt. It wasn't good enough. I supposed it would just have to do. Maybe I could tie-dye it.

"Suzy," announced Zed, with some significance.

We waited to hear what Zed might have to say about Suzy. Up above, great black clouds absorbed the neon light from the park. Zed lurched over towards the children's playground and fitted himself onto a swing that was much too small for him. He swung back and forth for a while.

"She wants me to go to university. The stupid bitch," he called, then laughed.

We laughed too. If Zed thought it was funny then so did we. But really it seemed unbelievable that even Zed could call Suzy a stupid bitch.

Zed started singing 'Whole Lotta Love', still playing on the child's swing.

He sang the riff as well. So did Greg and I. Da-da da-da DA da-da da-da… and on like that for a long time.

A group of older teenagers entered the park from the far end. They had cropped hair and boots. Knowing that they would not take kindly to us young hippies, Greg and I made to leave.

"It's okay," said Zed. "I know them."

None of the gang spoke to me but as I was with Zed, none of them gave me a hard time either. They respected Zed even though he was more outlandishly dressed than anyone else.

Later, Greg and I wondered about Zed calling Suzy a bitch.

"Think how upset she'd be if she knew."

Of course, we could not be so disloyal to Zed as to repeat his words to Suzy.

A train rumbled by in the distance. Greg and I pretended it was the sound of the Monstrous Hordes of Xotha. We were ready to fight for the future of mankind. The night of the gig was shaping up to be a decisive battle. Omens were everywhere to be seen. When Led Zeppelin arrived we were expecting Atlantis to rise from the bottom of the ocean.

twenty-eight

TICKETS FOR THE GIG went on sale on Friday the 10th of November, 1972, at the Clydesdale record shop on the corner of Sauchiehall Street and Rose Street. Here is part of a report from a newspaper of the time:

> Led Zeppelin, who are playing a 24 concert British tour next month, sold out 110,000 tickets within four hours of them going on sale. The queues formed early in most cities. All night queues formed in Glasgow's Sauchiehall Street despite freezing conditions and icy rain. Fans wrapped themselves in plastic sheets to keep warm, and hot soup was available.

So that is where I was on the night of Thursday the 9th, and morning of Friday the 10th of November. It certainly was freezing cold. I remember the icy rain, though I can't remember anyone bringing me hot soup. In fact, I'd swear they didn't.

I remember the police being there and facing the long queue of frozen young fans as if we were an invading army of violent criminals. At one point an Inspector opened the door of a police van, motioned inside and said, "there's plenty of room in there." There hadn't been any trouble, but in the seventies the police in Glasgow regarded young rock fans as their natural enemies.

I queued with Greg and Suzy. I had my grey air force greatcoat on, a popular choice with young hippies of the time. It had once been a warm coat, but now the lining was gone and there were rips in the seams. By midnight I was frozen through. Suzy was wearing her afghan. In Glasgow people bought their afghan coats at Millets which was, then as now, the sort of shop which normally sold camping equipment and comfy tartan shirts. I don't know why they also sold afghans.

Suzy huddled close to Greg and me, which was fine with us. Zed was also in the queue, but some way behind. He'd turned up with some older friends of his after an evening drinking in a student bar. He barely acknowledged Suzy and she looked away when he arrived.

We smoked cigarettes and waited for the night to pass. There wasn't any great spirit of joy in the queue. No singsongs of popular hits of the day for instance. It was too cold, and there was some nervousness that when dawn arrived the fans far back in the line might start a stampede and take our places. When daylight finally crawled around it was obvious that the queue, winding on and on from Sauchiehall Street down Cambridge Street and Renfrew Street, was made up of many more people than could fit into Green's Playhouse.

Sauchiehall. It always seemed like a strange name for a street. It comes from 'Saugh', which is an old Scottish word for a willow tree. By 1972, you would have been hard put to find any trees nearby, and any that were hanging on would have been half dead from traffic pollution.

After I left Glasgow, they smartened up the city centre, and planted a lot more trees. Most of Sauchiehall Street is a pedestrian precinct now. It looks a lot nicer.

At one point, some people got inside a canvas workman's tent, and started walking up and down so it looked like it was a tent with legs, which made everyone laugh.

"I'm so cold," said Suzy to me and Greg. "Put your arms round me."

We put our arms round her. It felt good. I avoided catching Greg's eye, not wanting to share the good feeling with him. Suzy was buying a ticket for Cherry. Greg and I found it hard to believe that Cherry was now a Led Zeppelin fan.

"It's because she's been writing love poems to Zed," suggested Greg.

"She'll steal Zed from you," I joked. The thought of Cherry going out with Zed made us all laugh, even Suzy, who wasn't feeling very humorous about Zed right then.

When the box office opened there wasn't a stampede. We entered in good order and bought our tickets, £1.00 each. I was numb with the cold. The parents of another friend of ours arrived to take her home and we all got a lift back to Bishopbriggs. When the numbness wore off I had raging pains in my ears and nose and mouth. The cold seemed to have entered my body and damaged it. It took a long time to wear off and I didn't go to school.

Next day, my picture was on the cover of a Glasgow newspaper, happily clutching my ticket. One of our teachers showed it to the class, with disapproval. However, I didn't get into trouble about it. I wouldn't have cared if I did. After all, with a Led Zeppelin ticket in my pocket, what would I have cared about some trouble at school? 'To hell with you all,' I would have said.

So now we had our tickets. Furthermore, Greg and I had seen proof that Suzy was not getting on at all well with Zed, and that was exciting.

"If they break up, Suzy will definitely need someone to comfort her," announced Greg. Greg sounded quite confident that he would be the person to provide her with comfort. For the first time I felt some annoyance at

Greg for being taller and better looking than me, and having longer hair, and being more confident. Why was it that Zed had given him the embroidered T-shirt? Why hadn't he given it to me? Greg wasn't any better friends with Zed than I was. At least I didn't think he was. Perhaps I had been wrong. I was very unhappy about the T-shirt.

twenty-nine

HUGE UNBROKEN BANKS OF DARK GREY CLOUDS hung over Glasgow as they had done for weeks without end. Sometimes we never saw the sun for month after month, just endless stretches of cloud and relentless heavy rain as the waters of the Atlantic Ocean evaporated into the sky for a brief journey over the west coast of Scotland before depositing themselves on Glasgow. Summer and winter, we had a lot of rain.

Lightning split the sky. I looked up and saw a huge Zeppelin flying overhead. I wasn't surprised. I expected there would be plenty more Zeppelins heading this way in the next few weeks, carrying the denizens of the Fantastic Lands to Glasgow to see the gig. This one was bringing Vikings and elvish armies to prepare the way. Sitting behind the Vikings was Jimi Hendrix, deceased in 1970, who was flying down to see how guitar music was getting on now that he'd gone.

Jimi turned to Sonny Boy Williamson, another passenger.

"Ever been in Glasgow before?"

Sonny Boy Williamson shook his head.

"The freight trains don't run this far."

In the wake of the airship came hordes of Scottish fairies.

"A huge Zeppelin full of mystical power. What does it mean?"

The fairies weren't sure, and flew closer to investigate.

I imagined that the Led Zeppelin gig would be an event of such cosmic importance that all sorts of spectacular events would occur as the various dimensions of the universe were thrown together. Atlantis would surely rise from the waves.

Plato wrote that Atlantis was an advanced civilisation situated in the Atlantic Ocean, some way west of the Straits of Gibraltar. It was once a utopia but when the people became degenerate the whole island sank beneath the ocean in a gigantic cataclysm. This happened 9,000 years before the time of Plato. The Egyptians kept records of it, and Plato learned the story from the descendants of Solon, a famous Athenian lawmaker who had travelled to Egypt.

I asked our teacher about this when she was getting us to do another project about Egypt, but our teacher had no interest in Atlantis.

There were a few survivors of the disaster. They lived in technologically advanced undersea domes, and flew out on their dragons to help Greg and me in our battles with the Monstrous Hordes of Xotha.

Led Zeppelin may have been responsible for my fixation with Atlantis. They were signed to Atlantic records. I thought that probably wasn't a coincidence.

thirty

WHEN ZED DIDN'T TURN UP AT SCHOOL for a few days it was rumoured he was in trouble, something to do with stealing a car. It turned out to be the car belonging to one of his friend's parents. The friend had been with him at the time, so it was more a case of teenage misbehaviour than grand theft auto. They'd taken the car without permission and driven out to the countryside at night although neither of them had a driving licence. It had ended badly when they were arrested by the police after running the car into a ditch.

This sort of thing was starting to happen to Zed more and more. Of course the more trouble he was in, the better Greg and I liked him. So did Suzy, up to a point. It was fun going out with a rebel. But I don't think Suzy really appreciated it when Zed took it to extremes. Suzy wasn't the sort of girl who was ever going to jump in a car and head off across the country just to see what was out there. She was keen to go to university, and that meant studying to pass her exams.

Zed was full of ambitions to travel to India and the USA. Suzy thought he should go to university first. They argued about this and I'd hear both sides of the story, as Suzy and Zed complained to me about each other. On occasion, I had to pass on some message of reconciliation which would bring them back into harmony. I liked the importance of doing this for such a significant couple as Zed and Suzy, but the irony of it didn't escape me. Helping them get back together was never going to get me into bed with Suzy. I hated being the dull friend that Suzy could confess her romantic secrets to.

Zed didn't have to go to court after the car theft. The detectives who arrested him, on learning that his father worked for the police, let him off with a warning. His father figured he had better do something about his errant son so he punched him around a little. Zed appeared at school with bruises on his face and a black eye which he hid behind a pair of pink-lensed granny glasses.

Zed's bruises didn't alert a social worker or anything like that. I don't think there were any social workers around at that time. There didn't seem to be anyone to protest about fathers beating their sons. It was probably regarded as good for their character.

After this episode, Suzy didn't know what to think. She wasn't pleased at the car escapade, but the trouble that Zed found himself in strengthened her feelings for him.

"You can't blame her for standing by her boyfriend," said Greg, wisely. "It's the right thing to do."

We scanned the skies for Zeppelins and dragons. I was thrown out of French class for not learning any French. Led Zeppelin was only twelve days away. I was feeling stranger and stranger. I was convinced I had a twitch but when I looked in the mirror nothing seemed to be twitching. It must just be some dangerous internal convulsions. Suzy came to school in new platform boots and I felt the convulsions getting worse. Her hair seemed to be getting longer and blonder every day. I developed a sort of lust-related asthma, and when I sat behind her in class I sometimes found it difficult to breathe properly.

I had now stopped eating and I'd lost weight. I was as thin as Zed and Greg. I was as thin as Jimmy Page. I wondered if Suzy had noticed.

Cherry appeared to have forgiven me for the diary outrage. She didn't have enough friends to stay angry at anyone for long. She caught up with me as I was walking to school.

"You've lost weight," she said.

I was pleased, pleased enough not to tell her to go away.

"Do you think so? Did Suzy notice?"

Cherry didn't know. She asked me if I was bothered if Suzy noticed?

"Of course," I said, though I realised that this was too revealing about my feelings for Suzy.

"I expect she noticed," said Cherry.

We got talking a little. Cherry was aware of all the difficulties between Suzy and Zed. To my surprise, she thought that Zed shouldn't go to university.

"I thought you'd support Suzy."

Cherry shrugged.

"Zed wants to go adventuring. He should do that. He can go to university later if he wants. A year or two won't make any difference."

That seemed sensible. It was a big surprise to hear Cherry say anything sensible. By now we were close to the school gates so I accelerated away, not wanting to let anyone see me arriving in her company. I still thought she was odd-looking. Only someone unattractive like Phil could possibly be in love with her.

I'd talked to Phil again. We met while he was out buying Sunday newspapers for his family. He was embarrassed about the episode of drunkenness and asked me not to tell anyone about it. However, his embarrassment didn't prevent him from raising the topic of Cherry. Not wishing to hear this, I told him that really it was nothing to do with me, but Phil became quite insistent. He didn't have anyone else to tell about it and it was eating him up inside.

"I knew she was in love with someone else. She writes love poems to a mysterious stranger called 'Z'. It must be Zed."

"It seems likely."

"Why would she like Zed better than me?"

That was a hard question to answer. There were hundreds of reasons for Cherry to like Zed better than Phil, but all of them would be hurtful. I felt sorry for Phil. I didn't want to be hurtful.

"I'm her best friend," said Phil.

He was wearing a grey sleeveless jumper over a grey shirt. It was ridiculous. How could you be in love in an outfit like that? Phil hated it that he was only friends with Cherry. He yearned for her to fall in love with him.

thirty-one

HERE IS HOW MANX GOT HER NEFERTITI HAT.

She had spent 1985 in India, 1986 in Thailand and 1992 in Vietnam. Manx was a very keen traveller.

"You should travel," she would say to her friends. "It's your planet. You should go and see it."

Next she planned to visit Nigeria, where one of her grandparents still lived.

When she was in London, Manx made a living partly by working in a picture library, partly by working as an assistant in a cafe at a small theatre, and partly by busking with a friend who juggled fire clubs and hoops.

She got the Nefertiti hat from the theatre when they had a sale of props. As she was working there at the time, she didn't even have to pay for it. They gave it to her for free. Manx was popular at the theatre.

"You want the hat, Manx? Just take it. It suits you."

"Look at Manx in the hat. She makes a great Nefertiti!"

Everyone liked Manx.

The company had the hat because they had once put on a play based on the life of Pharaoh Akhenaton, Nefertiti's husband. The hat was made by a prop maker in Brixton. The prop maker was Australian and, by chance, I knew her. So it turned out that the fabulous Nefertiti hat was actually constructed by someone I knew. Another of life's little coincidences, though I didn't realise this at the time.

Nefertiti means 'The Beautiful Woman Has Arrived'. It must have been nice having a name like that. Later she added 'Nefernefruaten' to her name. 'Nefernefruaten' means 'The Beautiful Woman Is Beautiful in the Sight of Aten'. Aten was a new God who was being worshipped at the time. The new religion was being promoted by Nefertiti and Akhenaton. It caused them terrible trouble with the conservative priesthood.

Manx was beautiful in her Nefertiti hat.

Manx is also a type of cat. It doesn't have a tail.

thirty-two

ONCE, IN THE DARK EARLY MORNING while Greg and I were out delivering newspapers, we discussed the nature of time, because the previous day we had been talking about time in physics class. When you got right down to it, time was very hard to understand. Nobel Prize winning scientists all over the world couldn't agree about the nature of time, so it was probably overly ambitious of our physics teacher to try it out on the class. We were baffled. Time was unfathomable.

I could step out right now and deliver newspapers with Greg, and take up the conversation where we left off all those years ago. I wouldn't notice that any time had passed.

Zed had been wearing a new T-shirt, one guaranteed to cause outrage in school. It had a picture of Nefertiti on it, altered so that she was smoking a joint. That was quite a popular motif for T-shirts in the seventies, some well-known figure with a joint hanging from their lips.

I never liked marijuana. Nefertiti, an altogether more rounded figure than myself, may well have enjoyed it had she had the opportunity. It might have relaxed her during the troubling times at court when the priesthood was in revolt over the religious reforms introduced by her and her husband Pharaoh Akhenaton.

Despite the widespread archaeological research that has been carried out in Egypt, Nefertiti's tomb has never been found. I'm glad about that. I'm pleased to know she is lying peacefully beneath the desert rather than being on display as a mummy in a museum.

It was an excellent T-shirt and it was because of this that Zed had given his embroidered T-shirt to Greg. That still rankled with me. I wondered if Zed had given it to Greg rather than me because his hair was longer than mine.

That led me on to other gloomy imaginings. If Suzy did break up with Zed and was looking round for a little comfort then Greg was surely the popular favourite. As well as being more attractive, he had a bigger record collection and he could play the guitar. He was an inch taller than Suzy. Greg seemed to have the upper hand in every department. All I had going for me was that I lived closer. If Suzy was really desperate for some comforting I could get to her first, but that was about it. Providing she could hold out for a few minutes longer, it seemed certain she would go with Greg.

I became anxious about this. Suzy with Zed made me miserable but Suzy with Greg would be a lot worse.

With no light on the horizon, I sat in my room listening to Led Zeppelin, and counted the days impatiently. For the past ten months or so I had been listening to *Led Zeppelin Four*. It was the best album in the world. *Led Zeppelin Two* was also the best album in the world but that was just one of these things about Led Zeppelin, they could defy the normal laws of space and time.

Led Zeppelin Four didn't have a title. It wasn't really called *Led Zeppelin Four*. No one knew what it was called. All it had on the cover was some weird symbols. We were impressed. No one else would have thought of doing that. It seemed that every action they took served only to emphasise the great genius of Led Zeppelin. They could put out a record that didn't even have a title and it was still the best record in the world.

The first song on the album is 'Black Dog'. I have sung the words to the introduction quietly to myself for the last twenty-seven years, imagining that I, like Robert Plant, might make some beautiful woman sweat and groove. Of course, I can't sing it like Robert Plant. I hum the riff as well, but this can be quite difficult. It starts off easy enough but then it gets really complicated in the middle section. After years of practice, I still can't get it exactly right.

With the release of *Led Zeppelin Four,* 'Stairway to Heaven' had now been let loose in the world. This went on to be their most popular song. It received millions of radio plays and became familiar even to people who had never heard anything else by Led Zeppelin. All over the world, young guitarists walking into music shops to check out the new guitars, would strum the first few chords of 'Stairway to Heaven'.

The song became so popular that people eventually became sick of it. They began to hate it, to revile it in a manner quite unusual for a piece of music. 'Stairway to Heaven' acquired the status of public enemy. I couldn't see that coming. I have never been any good at forecasting the future. I didn't have the slightest inkling that one day 'Stairway to Heaven' would be widely disliked. Nor did I foresee that Billy Myers, who sat next to me in physics class, was going to die of leukaemia. There didn't seem to be any warning. One day he had a sore throat, the next day he was in hospital and the next day he was dead. People are so fragile. Sometimes I wonder how anyone ever grows up at all.

thirty-three

I SAVED UP MY PAPER ROUND MONEY to buy posters and after a while I had nine large images of Led Zeppelin pinned to my bedroom wall. I used pins because blu-tac had not yet been invented. Or if it had been invented, it hadn't reached Glasgow. A world without blu-tac. Imagine that.

Some of those posters were copies of original advertisements. One announced a gig in January 1969, at the Filmore East in New York where they had played with Iron Butterfly and the Move. The poster also mentioned other nights at the same venue featuring Janis Joplin, Canned Heat and the Grateful Dead. Tickets were $3.

My favourite poster was an advert for their gig at the Empire Pool in London, November 1971. "Buffalo Concert Presentations in Association with Peter Grant presents Electric Magic featuring Led Zeppelin." I treasured this brightly coloured poster. It seemed to me like a very psychedelic item, with its bold lettering in red, yellow and green, and Jimmy Page swathed in a red cloak like a musical saint from a stained glass window. A streaming galaxy of stars flowed round the band, giving heavenly haloes to Jimmy Page and John Paul Jones, and there were stars on the shirts of Robert Plant and John Bonham. The mystic symbols from the sleeve of the fourth album were prominently displayed and, rather than modern instruments, Jimmy Page and John Paul Jones were holding lutes, which added a feeling of mediaeval mystery. At the foot of the picture a magician held out his arms, ready to cast the electric magic.

The drawing of Jimmy Page showed him with a beard, which was rare. Led Zeppelin were generally clean-shaven, but every one of them experimented with a beard for at least a short time. John Bonham was most often bearded, and he usually had a moustache. John Bonham was a builder's labourer before he was a drummer, which is how he developed such powerful arms.

Years later, I found a T-shirt emblazoned with this same poster. I bought it immediately, though it didn't have all the original colours, just black, white and red. I liked it anyway.

I still have it. I'm wearing it to write this book. It's years since I wore a T-shirt with a band's name on it. It feels good.

My other posters were press photos of the band performing. I had three pictures showing them all on stage, one that was just Jimmy Page and two that were just Robert Plant.

Although Jimmy Page and Robert Plant were the most prominent members, I didn't ignore the others. Every year I filled in the forms in all the music papers to vote for my favourite musicians in all categories and I was always pleased to send away my votes for John Paul

Jones as the best bass guitarist and John Bonham as the best drummer.

Led Zeppelin had been successful right from their beginnings in 1969. By 1971 they'd already taken over the world. It was no longer possible for them to play in small clubs. Even the 4,000 seat Green's Playhouse was far below the capacity of the American venues they would visit.

I looked at the images on my walls and wished that I was older, that I was seeing Led Zeppelin in Vancouver or New York or London instead of being stuck in school in Glasgow, failing to learn French, being picked on by bullies, and aching about Suzy.

The summer before, I'd gone into the centre of Glasgow with Suzy to visit the poster shop. It was July and we were on holiday from school. We walked around town for a while, along Sauchiehall Street, down Union Street to Argyle Street. The centre of town was crowded, a pleasant place with wide streets and stone buildings four or five stories high. Shops on the ground floor, apartments or office space above them. The stone was black from years of car fumes. Later they were cleaned up and became honey-coloured, or grey.

We looked through the records. At this time Suzy had not started her Saturday job. Her parents didn't give her any money so she couldn't buy anything. I only had enough for the poster I wanted, but we liked to peruse the records anyway. Hawkwind, Black Sabbath, things we liked. We didn't like the Velvet Underground. Too arty, and not enough power chords. And I'd stand by that judgement to this day.

The man behind the counter in the poster section had a huge black beard and rimless glasses, wore dungarees and a Keep On Truckin' T-shirt and was the most hippyish person anywhere in Glasgow. We imagined that he smoked dope in the back of the shop, and we were probably correct. He certainly spent a lot of time looking vacantly into the distance.

I was buying the Led Zeppelin 'Empire Pool' poster. The assistant took a long time to find it, roll it up and put it in a tube, and even longer to take my money.

Money had recently changed. Britain had adopted a decimal system of currency and there were now 100 pennies in a pound. Only a few months ago there had been 240. It was confusing for a while.

"It's a good poster," said Suzy.

Something in her voice struck me as a little odd. Wistful perhaps? I wondered if Suzy wanted me to buy her a poster. She didn't have any money to buy her own. Neither did I, now I'd bought this. I felt at a bit of a loss.

Later I asked Greg about it.

"Do you think Suzy might have wanted me to give her my poster?"

Greg didn't know. The way women in Led Zeppelin songs were often wanting diamonds and pearls, it was possible. But even here, it wasn't clear cut. Greg was astute enough to realise that the women in Led Zeppelin's old blues numbers were sometimes different to the women in their more modern creations. The world was changing. Women were becoming independent. Led Zeppelin's newer women seemed to like lying around in the sun, smoking dope and being free. They might not like being given presents any more.

It was a dilemma. Anyway, I loved my new poster. I didn't want to give it away.

"Why do you think Zed gave his embroidered T-shirt to Greg instead of me?" I asked Suzy, as we waited for the bus home. "Does he like him better?"

"Probably," replied Suzy, and laughed.

thirty-four

ZED HAD AN AFGHAN COAT. So had Suzy. John, a student friend of Zed's, had an afghan coat. These were all people I admired. I wanted to dress like them but my morning paper round was never going to earn me enough to buy a coat like theirs.

I seemed to be meeting Cherry more often as I walked to school. She told me she'd like an afghan coat too but her parents wouldn't allow it. I mentioned how fabulous Suzy looked in hers.

"Suzy always looks fabulous," said Cherry.

We carried on in silence for a while.

"Do you think I should get a new pair of glasses?" asked Cherry

"Yes," I told her. "These ones are terrible."

I walked on, thinking about how much I wanted an afghan coat. I never did get one. I regret this.

I did once live in a friend's flat for a few months while she was in Poland making a film. In her flat, secreted at the back of a wardrobe, I found a real fur coat. By this time a fur coat was a shameful thing to have in the sort of circles I moved in. Everyone was against killing animals and wearing their fur. Even being suspected of having such a thing would have led to social ostracism. No wonder the fur coat was hidden.

I kept well away from the garment. Yes, I can honestly say that apart from occasionally wearing it as a dressing gown, sometimes wrapping it round me when the nights were getting cold, once or twice trying it on just to see what it looked like in the full-length mirror, and a few times having sex with my girlfriend while wearing it, I never went near the fur coat.

By the time I was old enough to buy my own afghan,

they'd gone terminally out of style. No rational person could have gone and bought one. I remain frustrated about this. If I do readings from my Led Zeppelin book, I'll find one in a hippy shop somewhere and wear it while reading. I will tour the country in an afghan coat. No one can stop me.

"Why do you think Zed gave his embroidered T-shirt to Greg instead of me?" I asked Cherry. "Does he like him better?"

"I don't think so," replied Cherry. "I think it probably just fits him better than you. Greg's the same size as Zed."

This hadn't occurred to me. It seemed plausible. Possibly Cherry was not the total idiot I took her for.

"Your glasses aren't really that terrible," I said to her, by way of consolation.

thirty-five

ZED'S PARENTS WERE AWAY and we were going round to his house to hang out and listen to records. Suzy said we had to wait for Cherry. We were displeased that Cherry was to accompany us.

"She'll embarrass us. Zed won't like it if we bring her. What if she starts writing a poem or something?"

"How's Zed going to feel if people learn that Cherry the freak has been at his house?"

Suzy said that she had checked with Zed and it was fine with him. Suzy had to take Cherry because she owed her a favour. Cherry had written an essay for her.

"Did Cherry write the whole essay?"

"Yes. Then I copied it and handed it in. I got an A. So I owe her."

Greg and I were impressed. It showed high intelligence on Suzy's part to get Cherry to do her essays for her. We were still dubious about taking her to Zed's. People might start saying she was our friend. Our social status, already very low, would plummet further.

"Could you encourage her to not wear her glasses?" suggested Greg. "And maybe get rid of her freckles?"

"If she wears her school blazer I'm not walking with her," I stated, quite firmly, and I meant it.

Cherry wasn't wearing her school blazer. She appeared in a bright new Led Zeppelin T-shirt. Greg and I were unhappy at this. We had liked the band for ages. We didn't want Cherry muscling in on the act with a brand new T-shirt. The girl seemed determined to spoil everything.

"Nice T-shirt," said Greg.

Cherry looked pleased but when she saw that Greg was being sarcastic her face fell. Suzy hustled us out of the house and we went round to Zed's. There were six days left till the gig.

thirty-six

IN 1972, ROCK MUSICIANS were rarely written about by the straight press. They never made it into gossip columns or appeared on television. Radio stations in Britain hardly ever played their records. Even though Led Zeppelin were the biggest band in the world, it was quite possible that many of their fans' parents had never heard of them. So it seemed that they belonged only to us, and that felt important. It made everything better.

The legal age for buying alcohol in Scotland was eighteen, but most places in Glasgow insisted that you be twenty-one. That made things awkward for young drinkers, but there were ways round it. No doubt you will be familiar with these. Persuading an older friend or relative to buy drink for you seems to be a universal experience.

No alcohol was allowed in Green's Playhouse so people from my school would consume whole carrier bags full of cans of McEwan's Export in the short space between Buchanan Street bus garage and the theatre, often with distressing results.

The bouncers were not friendly. They would take pleasure in ramming people back into their seats, or even throwing them out of the auditorium altogether. At a large gig like Led Zeppelin they were powerless to do that; the crowd were too frenzied to be controlled. The security men would just retreat to the front of the stage and stare out at the audience, hostile and uncomprehending, not understanding why all those young people were so excited.

Despite the hostility of the staff, we were not searched on the way in. In those days it was unusual to be searched. It was not difficult to take in bottles of soft drink laced with alcohol, and many people did that. So when Led Zeppelin came on stage the audience was already fuelled with liquor. Parts of the audience were no doubt fuelled with drugs, though I was too naive to realise it at the time.

The lights went down and the audience howled. Even at that late stage I wouldn't have been surprised to hear an announcement that the gig had been cancelled. I could be quite determined in my pessimism.

The band walked on in this order: Robert Plant, Jimmy Page, John Paul Jones, John Bonham. The crowd rose to their feet, and started screaming. I was an enthusiastic screamer. People started running to the front and, before a note had been played, the bouncers found themselves forced back as far as they could go.

I looked at Led Zeppelin, standing on the stage, here in Glasgow at last. Already I felt satisfied. I wasn't attractive. I never would be. I'd never get the girl I wanted. I didn't have any money. I didn't have many friends. I'd never had sex. I was in trouble at school. I knew my life would never go well. I was quite a miserable kid but hey, what the hell. Led Zeppelin were now about to play and I was there, climbing over rows of seats to get nearer, and screaming at them to let them know I loved them.

thirty-seven

I'M OUT WITH MANX, walking through part of the covered market in Brixton. Manx is pushing her baby in a buggy which makes for slow progress in the confined and crowded area. I look at the stalls full of exotic fish, which are interesting.

"They didn't have any exotic fish when I was growing up in Glasgow," I tell Manx. "Just cod and haddock."

"Maybe it's time you experimented."

"No. Something bad would happen. I'd be as well just swallowing a capsule of cyanide."

Manx will eat any kind of fish. Manx is a great adventurer. She's travelled the world.

Hidden at the back of a stall, unwanted, I notice a small cheesecloth shirt. I point it out enthusiastically to Manx.

"It's horrible," she says. "You only like it because it reminds you of being fourteen."

I have to admit this is true.

"Still, Manx, you used to wear something quite a lot like it. Around the same time you were wearing the Nefertiti hat."

"Please don't mention the hat."

"It was a terrific hat. You should wear it."

Manx makes a face.

"Ask me again when I'm not the world's most boring person."

Manx is really putting herself down these days. I'm worried.

What I mainly remember about my cheesecloth shirt is that the buttons were small and the buttonholes lost their shape so it was always coming undone. It was a very Led Zeppelin type of garment.

Manx departs to the library to look for some books on computer programming. She is making little progress with her animation and it's worrying her. I've asked her if she would like to help me judge the literary competition and she says she would, if she has time.

thirty-eight

NEXT DAY MANX IS UPSET WITH ME.

"I can't believe you slept with Jane," she says, indignantly.

"She was lonely. She needed a friend."

"A friend? You don't even like her."

"Liking someone has no relation to sleeping with them," I point out. "I've never found that disliking a person makes any difference at all to finding them attractive. It might even be an aphrodisiac."

"You disgust me."

"But fortunately not Jane. She arrived here depressed, and left a happy woman. Well maybe not happy, but I swear she was more cheerful. Anyway, you're mistaken about me disliking her. It's the Jane who's depressed because she thinks she's overweight I don't like. You know, the skinny one. The woman I spent last night cheering up is the Jane who's always depressed for no reason.'

"Oh that Jane," says Manx. "I remember her. It's lucky that Prozac isn't as good as it's made out to be or you'd never get any sex at all. Have you ever slept with anyone who wasn't a mental case?"

I think about this.

"Not for some time. But it's not my fault. I can't help it if all the women I meet are bulimic, anorexic, agoraphobic, schizophrenic, clinically depressed, manically depressed, full of self-loathing, self destructive, suicidal, or otherwise struggling to find a reason to keep on living. I don't know what's the matter with them all."

"This doesn't prevent you from luring them into bed by listening to their problems."

I admit that this is true. I have often benefited from the problems of my female friends.

"But I didn't cause their problems. It's society that does the damage. I'm just here to pick up the pieces. And you could say I provide a valuable service to the community. After all, no one wants to commit suicide while they're actually fucking. Well almost no one. Pauline was a special case, and it wasn't just with me. And I always make a nice breakfast in the morning. I'm full of consideration."

It's true. I am. And I am an excellent listener. I learned this at school, from listening to Suzy. She told me that Zed wanted to leave school and go to London and he wanted Suzy to go with him. Surprisingly, Suzy did not altogether dismiss the idea. She loved Zed but her parents objected to him. It was causing arguments at home. Maybe just moving away wasn't such a bad idea.

I thought it was a terrible idea, but I didn't like to say so for fear of appearing dull. So I just listened, and looked at her eyes, which were slightly oriental in appearance.

Suzy. Blonde and feline. I never met anyone else who looked quite like her. She had a soft voice. And very neat handwriting. And few delusions, as far as I could tell. She always seemed quite realistic about her life.

Of course anyone can have delusions. For a long time I believed that on the night of the 14th of November, 1972, a real Zeppelin flew over Glasgow. It hovered over Renfield Street, right next to Green's Playhouse. I stared up in wonderment, and hoped that it wasn't going to crash in flames like the airship on the cover of Led Zeppelin's first album.

For years, I was convinced that a Zeppelin flew over Glasgow that night. Not till I mentioned it to a friend, and she looked at me in a certain kind of way, did it even strike me as strange. When I actually thought about it, I had to admit it was unlikely.

"It might have been there," I said out loud, quite defiantly. "It could have been advertising the gig."

By this time, I only had one friend left who still lived in Glasgow. I called him up.

"You remember the Led Zeppelin gig? Did a real Zeppelin fly over Glasgow? I seem to remember it hovering over Green's Playhouse."

My friend burst out laughing.

"Of course a Zeppelin didn't fly over Glasgow," he said. "Were you stoned?"

"No. I never had any drugs when I was that age. But I remember it. It was caught in the searchlights."

"There weren't any searchlights."

"No searchlights?"

"No."

It was depressing to realise that for all those years I had imagined a mighty airship welcoming me to the gig. A huge Zeppelin floating majestically over Glasgow which only I had seen. Something of a mental aberration, I had to admit.

The carpet at Green's Playhouse had words woven into it. They said: 'It's Green's, It's Good.' That is undoubtedly true. Other people remember it.

thirty-nine

I GO TO THE SUPERMARKET WITH MANX, but the way I have to read the ingredients of everything, checking for poisonous preservatives and harmful chemicals, has started to aggravate her.

"Why do you check the ingredients every time you buy a loaf of bread?"

"In case they've changed."

I can't help it. I'm just suspicious about food. Manx isn't so suspicious about it but it still makes her depressed. She hasn't been eating well. She buys baby supplies and we head for the check-out.

The shopping trolley runs smoothly, and straight. They've really improved the design of shopping trolleys these days. It's progress. We wait for a short time at the check-out.

"Since they got the bar codes sorted out you get through the check-out a lot quicker."

"It's true," says Manx. "There's no denying it, this supermarket is loads better than it used to be."

Despite this we don't seem to have managed to buy any food for ourselves. I worry about Manx. She's not eating enough.

We catch a bus back to my house to watch cable TV. Stone Cold Steve Austin is battling it out for the World Wrestling Federation Championship with the Undertaker, the hugely muscled and heavily tattooed nemesis of the ring. The Undertaker wins, but only with the help of some gross cheating by his henchman who makes a shocking assault on the referee. The crowd is furious.

"Don't worry," I tell baby Malachi. "Stone Cold Steve Austen will be back for another attempt soon. No one gets the better of him for long."

"I never knew wrestling was so interesting," says Manx.

"It's because it's American. British TV has really gone downhill. We have nothing to compete with this sort of thing."

I hurry around making tea and getting cups and milk and biscuits so we can settle down and watch *Buffy the Vampire Slayer* without interruption. *Buffy* is fantastic. It's the best programme ever made. I love *Buffy*.

I pass Manx a cup of tea.

"Now that British TV is so bad," I tell Manx, "it's really putting me off Shakespeare and the classics. I mean, if we can't make a decent TV programme any more, what's the point of defending our culture? I can't do everything myself. I am defecting across the Atlantic to Buffyland."

"Good tea," says Manx

My tea is always good. You have to make it in a pot, let it brew, and put the milk in the cups first. However, not many people do this now. In restaurants, and even friends' houses, you're quite likely just to get a tea bag dumped in a cup. Most people in Britain have forgotten how to make a proper cup of tea. Useless television and bad tea. The nation is in chaos. It's a shambles.

Buffy is fabulous. So is her friend Willow. I rarely bothered with TV when I was at school. I needed all my time for listening to Led Zeppelin.

forty

I ONCE MET SOMEONE who claimed to have been working as a roadie at the gig in Glasgow. That was years later, in London. I wasn't sure whether to believe him or not. He was fairly messed up with drugs and that made him unreliable. You couldn't trust him not to steal your possessions. He might have been lying about being a roadie in Glasgow.

However, there was no denying that he was an excellent guitarist with a keen ear. He could play a lot of Led Zeppelin's music and did a particularly fine version of Jimmy Page's guitar break on 'When the Levee Breaks'.

This has always been one of my favourite songs. While it didn't immediately stand out on an album which contained 'Black Dog', 'Rock and Roll' and 'Stairway to Heaven', it was obviously a great tune and it has aged well. Its reputation grew in later years because of John Bonham's thundering drum sound.

Led Zeppelin recorded it in Hampshire at a large manor house called Headly Grange, and they got the drum sound when the engineer hung microphones down from the ceiling in the cavernous hallway. The lyrics were inspired by an old blues song by Memphis Minnie and Kansas Joe McCoy. Whilst on the face of it 'When the Levee Breaks' is a song about being worried about a flood of water washing away a dam, it is also a metaphor for a rising torrent of sexual desire, which threatens at any moment to overwhelm both the singer and the listener and carry them off into some wayward, abandoned, enjoyable but undoubtedly sinful behaviour. Despite never being the most astute interpreter of lyrics, I recognised this the first time I heard it, and at the age of thirteen and fourteen it was painfully appropriate. Sexual desire for Suzy was building up in a way that was fast becoming unendurable. Unfortunately, the song didn't seem to offer any solutions to the problem. At the end of it, Robert Plant seems to be on the point of giving the whole thing up and moving to Chicago. For me, stuck in Glasgow with maths books to read and newspapers to deliver, that didn't seem possible. Every day I'd see Suzy and be overwhelmed by this hopeless, crazed feeling which lay in some unidentifiable adolescent region between lust, romance, misery, joy and total desperation.

I wrapped my greatcoat around me to keep out the freezing wind and rain and tramped home after an evening with Zed, wondering if I would ever spend a night with Suzy and kicking stones in the same way that I had done when I was at primary school.

I hummed the tune and sang the words in my head, and wished that I could play guitar like Jimmy Page. Then, I presumed, women like Suzy would seek me out, enabling me to do something about the massive build-up of water on the other side of the dam, apart from just drowning in it.

Some years later, I did learn to play guitar, very badly. I never progressed much past the first three chords as demonstrated in *Sniffing Glue,* the original punk fanzine. *Sniffing Glue* was not keen on Led Zeppelin, though they gave a good farewell to Elvis Presley when he died.

My three chords never attracted any women. Even now, I'd still like to be able to play Jimmy Page's guitar part on 'When the Levee Breaks'.

forty-one

ZED WELCOMED US INTO HIS HOUSE. Led Zeppelin were playing, one of the tapes Zed had made from their radio sessions a few years ago. The track was 'Travelling Riverside Blues', which never appeared on an album and wasn't officially released for another twenty-five years, when the BBC finally issued the old recordings on a CD.

We sat amongst Zed's Led Zeppelin ephemera: the tapes from the radio sessions, his bootleg LPs from Baltimore and Tokyo. The walls of his room were covered with posters and magazine articles. One review from an underground magazine said that in the first track of the first album Jimmy Page did things with the guitar which were previously unheard of. I liked that.

"Nice T-shirt," said Zed to Cherry, without being sarcastic.

Cherry looked pleased, but, overcome by shyness, was unable to reply.

With only six days left to the gig, even Zed's excitement was starting to show. As he talked animatedly about the event, he seemed more like Greg and me. Suzy remained cool. She never got over-excited about anything.

We just couldn't wait. Robert Plant was going to appear and sing 'Stairway to Heaven'. Zed leapt to put on 'Stairway to Heaven' so we could imagine it happening, and he pretended to be Robert Plant. We plunged into a joint fantasy that we were watching them play in front of us. Zed made an excellent Robert Plant. He made an excellent Jimmy Page as well. He was talented like that.

"Could I make some tea?" said Cherry.

"Sure," said Zed, a little startled at having to drag himself back from his Robert Plant impersonation.

Cherry was fourteen and looked younger.

"I'll be fifteen by the time of the gig," she'd told us, eagerly. I'd already noticed she had a knack of saying exactly the wrong thing. Only a person of low sensitivity would have enquired about tea so early in Zed's Robert Plant impersonation. She hurried off to the kitchen.

Suzy was sixteen and looked older. She sat on the couch and held Zed's hand.

"I'm sorry about bringing Cherry," she said.

"Don't worry about it," said Zed. "I like her."

Zed lived in the same sort of house as I did. A large part of Bishopbriggs was made up of private housing estates, Wimpy houses as we called them, after the name of the constructor. These were small semi-detached buildings. Semi-detached means there are two of them stuck together. They were all quite similar, some larger than others but all with grey pebble-dash walls, a red tiled roof and a small garden at the back. Up the hill from us was Auchinairn, with a large expanse of council houses, also semi-detached.

I never thought much about Bishopbriggs, apart from it was a boring place, where nothing happened and there was nothing to do. Years later, after I had moved to London and had books published, I went back to Glasgow to do a reading. At the end, people asked questions.

"Are the council estates in your books about Brixton the same as the council estates in Glasgow?" someone inquired.

I replied that no, they were different, but anyway I'd never lived in a council estate in Glasgow. I'd grown up in a semi-detached house in Bishopbriggs. At which the audience laughed, the implication being that Bishopbriggs was a rather wealthy place to grow up, and not really like Glasgow at all. You can't argue with that.

Cherry arrived back from the kitchen with a pot of tea and a toy robot. I groaned. There seemed to be no uncool behaviour this girl was not capable of. We were here to listen to Led Zeppelin and talk about the gig, not play with toy robots.

"Does it work?" she asked.

Zed shook his head.

"Where did you get it?"

Zed looked uncomfortable, which I could understand. Even the coolest boy in the school doesn't want young girls asking him about his toys.

"A present from my uncle," he muttered. "It never worked."

We all looked pointedly at Cherry, trying to let her know that this was not an appropriate topic of conversation. Cherry didn't notice, and started examining the robot from all angles, pushing it along the floor, trying to get its lights to flash.

We discussed who else was going to the gig. Suzy's cousin Colin was going.

"He doesn't like them. But he doesn't want to miss the occasion."

Jenny, a friend of Zed's who worked in a flower shop in town, was going. Not only that, she was preparing flower arrangements for the dressing room.

"If she can hang around doing the flowers for long enough, she might get to meet the band."

We knew a lot of people who had tickets; friends at school, and all the university students that Zed knew. Suzy's friend Isobel was coming down from Inverness and bringing her thirteen-year-old brother with her.

"Can't you get it fixed?" said Cherry, brandishing the robot. Greg and I pursed our lips in frustration. To be fair to Cherry, it was quite an impressive toy. It hadn't come from a shop. Zed's uncle had made it at his workshop as a birthday present, years ago.

Zed shrugged.

"It never worked," he said.

Cherry's harping on about the robot was making Zed uncomfortable. I cursed her mentally, and changed the subject back to Led Zeppelin.

"Do you think they'll play 'Communication Breakdown'? I heard they dropped it from their set."

"They still use it as an encore," stated Zed, knowledgeably.

On the way home, Greg berated Cherry for being such an idiot.

"Why did you have to keep going on about the toy robot? It was making Zed uncomfortable."

Cherry was upset and looked very close to tears. We didn't comfort her.

Later, Suzy told Greg and me that she thought Zed might have been uncomfortable about the robot not because it was a childish toy but because his father had promised to get it fixed but never bothered. It had lain around broken for years, ever since Zed was small.

forty-two

I SAT WITH GREG AT NIGHT IN THE PARK. Suddenly, we were confronted by three youths who appeared out of the darkness and stared at us. I was nervous. They obviously weren't friendly. They came up and stood with their faces close to ours.

"Any cigarettes?"

Greg and I shook our heads. The youths started going through our pockets, which was humiliating, though I didn't mind too much if we escaped without being beaten up. They found cigarettes on both Greg and me, and took them, and our matches, along with the few coins we had on us. One of the youths fingered Greg's embroidered T-shirt and made some mocking remarks about it. No one with any self-respect would let some stranger stand there and abuse him in this way. Apart from me and Greg. We made no attempt to start a fight. We were never any good at fighting and would just have been beaten up.

Seeing that we were so completely helpless they started to lose interest. There wasn't much point in beating us up. They walked off into the darkness, lighting our cigarettes.

One of them called back over his shoulder.

"Spastics," he said.

'Spastic' was a popular term of abuse.

Greg and I were left without any dignity and turned to go. There, watching from the road by the park, were Cherry and Suzy. Greg and I were crushed. We didn't care very much that we were unable to defend ourselves against tough boys, and we could take this sort of occurrence philosophically, but not with our friends looking on. Not with Suzy watching, who we were in love with, and wanted to impress. Not with Cherry watching, who we now hated more than ever for seeing our weakness.

"There were three of them," mumbled Greg, trying to imply that, had we not been outnumbered, we would have put up some resistance. It sounded lame. I didn't make any excuses.

Both Suzy and Cherry were sympathetic. It didn't make us feel any better. As it was impossible to have any bad feelings against Suzy, I took them out on Cherry and was rude to her before going off home on my own to sit in my bedroom and listen to Led Zeppelin. I put on their third album which, with its many acoustic numbers, was quite calming. Led Zeppelin might occasionally pretend to be Viking warriors but more often they just liked to sing love songs, or sex songs. That was fine with me. I never expected much more than that from a song.

No one ever mentioned the incident again but I was humiliated about it for a long time. I tried pretending to myself that, rather than some youths, I had been robbed by a whole fire-breathing regiment of the Monstrous Hordes of Xotha but it didn't really make it better.

I wondered if the members of Led Zeppelin had been bullied at school. Maybe, though I couldn't really imagine it. They wouldn't have to worry about it now anyway. These days they had Peter Grant to protect them. Peter Grant was their manager, a massive man with a fierce reputation. He always kept them safe. And he earned them a lot of money with his shrewd negotiating skills.

'Spastic' was not only an insult. The word was still used to describe a person who had cerebral palsy. There was a charity called the Spastics Society. Later, as the word went out of use, the charity changed its name to the Cerebral Palsy Association. However, 'spastic' remained a common insult for a long time.

forty-three

I'D BOUGHT MY LED ZEPPELIN ticket on the 10th of November. The gig was on the 4th of December. Towards the end of November I was feeling very unwell. The stress was getting to me. I still couldn't believe that they would actually show up. It did happen more than once that bands I had a ticket for didn't appear. If the Led Zeppelin gig was cancelled I knew I wouldn't be able to bear it.

I read in the *NME* that the band had been in fine form in Japan and had played a triumphant date in Tokyo. Their tour of America earlier in the year had been immensely successful and in New York they'd played to a crowd of 16,000. Figures like that stuck in my mind. In Boston they appeared in front of 20,000 people. Twenty-five thousand had travelled from all parts of New Zealand to see them in Auckland.

Green's Playhouse couldn't compete with that sort of figure. It was said that the Playhouse had once been the largest cinema in Europe, seating 4,000 people. It seemed smaller than that to me. Some of the balconies were now blocked off and I'd guess that by 1972 the capacity for concerts was no more than 3,000. That wasn't much of an audience by Led Zeppelin's standards. What if they decided it wasn't worth travelling all the way to Glasgow just to play to 3,000 people? It might happen. Why come and play in Glasgow when they could be lounging around in California with swimming pools and movie starlets?

Neither Greg, Zed or Suzy seemed to share my worries.

"Of course they'll come? Why wouldn't they?"

If I was more pessimistic than most, I wasn't the only one gripped with feverish excitement. Last weekend in the record shop I'd seen a bunch of kids standing at the Led Zeppelin section, taking the record covers out of the rack, looking at them, discussing them, putting them back in the box then taking them out and starting the whole process over again. From their conversation it was obvious that they owned these records already and were all going to the gig. But they just wanted to stand there and touch the covers as some communal means of getting closer to the band.

Zed had now stopped going to school. Whether his parents didn't know, didn't mind, or didn't care, I wasn't sure, but right then he just stopped turning up. Sometimes in the day Greg and I would miss school and visit him. He seemed to have the run of the house to himself. He even drank beer from the fridge, a quite unheard-of piece of grown up behaviour.

"How are things between you and Suzy?" we asked.

Zed shrugged. He didn't seem bothered about it.

Zed had a strange piece of news. Cherry had called round, uninvited, and asked if she could take the robot away.

"She wants to see if she can fix it."

That baffled us. The girl seemed to be obsessed with Zed's robot.

"She's in love with you," said Greg to Zed, trying to tease him.

Suzy was not pleased when she learned about this. It was one thing to have her young companion writing poems which might possibly have been about Zed – opinion was still divided on the subject – but not so good to have her actively pursuing him.

"It's only to be expected that a hopeless case like Cherry might harbour secret longings for someone like Zed," said Suzy. "But that doesn't mean I want her hanging round him."

"I expect Zed thinks it's funny," suggested Greg, which cheered Suzy up.

It didn't seem to me that Zed had found it funny. I thought he had seemed pleased. I couldn't understand it. How could Zed like Cherry when she was quite plainly such a geek? Cherry was no better now than she had ever been. She might have a Led Zeppelin T-shirt but she still wore her terrible school blazer and had ridiculous glasses and fuzzy red hair. I might have mellowed towards her sufficiently to tell her how unhappy I was about Suzy, but I would never let her join the Fabulous Dragon Army.

Phil accosted me in the street as I returned from school and asked me if it was true that Cherry had gone with Greg and me to visit Zed. When I confirmed that it was, he looked crushed.

"I encourage her to write poems," he said. "No one else does. How come she doesn't like me the way she likes Zed?"

forty-four

I KEEP DESCRIBING MYSELF AND GREG AS HIPPIES. This is not strictly accurate. What we were was two schoolboys with long hair, flared jeans and T-shirts. We didn't subscribe to any hippy philosophy, or read books about San Francisco or study Eastern religions. We didn't plan to set up a commune when we left school, or chant for peace in St George's Square. We didn't even much like the great hippy bands like Jefferson Airplane or the Grateful Dead, because their music wasn't fierce enough. All we were doing really was copying the clothes of the people we saw in the music papers.

I assumed then that people were like this everywhere. But it was now five years after the great hippy explosion of 1967, so perhaps people in more fashionable places like London had moved on to other things. But we still liked to think of ourselves as hippies, if only because it made us feel like outsiders, and rebellious.

I did learn something about Eastern religion later on in life. I learned about Taoism in Tai Chi Chuan classes, and Buddhism in a meditation class. They were both interesting, but I doubt if either would have sustained me in my youth when I was frantic about Suzy and Led Zeppelin. I didn't want to be calmed down, I wanted to be in the midst of some frenzied sexual excesses.

December was bitterly cold. I wrapped myself up in my greatcoat and walked round to Suzy's house. Greg was already there. I was surprised. Greg hadn't called me to tell me he'd be visiting her. Normally he would have.

Suzy was sewing a piece of flower patterned material into her trousers, making the flares wider. I looked on, interested.

"I'm making them for the gig," Suzy explained. "What are you wearing?"

I looked blank. I hadn't thought about it. I didn't really have anything to wear.

"I want to do that," said Greg, indicating the newly emerging flower pattered flares.

"So do I," I said.

So Suzy showed us how to sew, and we wondered about what sort of material we could use to make our flares better. Suzy offered us some flower-patterned cotton but we rejected that as being too girly. We were derided enough without suddenly appearing with flowers on our trousers.

"Then just cut a piece of denim from an old pair of jeans and fit it in," suggested Suzy.

We liked that suggestion.

Suzy had a poster of Jimmy Page wearing black flares with embroidered patterns all down the sides. They were a fine pair of pants, the sort of thing you could only really wear if you were a big rock star. We couldn't turn up to the gig in anything like that but at least if our flares were wide enough, we wouldn't be completely disgraced.

Suzy also had a new array of make up, most of it Miner's, which she bought at Boots. Miner's was a common brand of make up for girls at my school. Also, she had some Rimmel blusher with little sparkly bits in it which she was planning on wearing to the gig. She'd been saving money from her new Saturday job in a newsagents to buy extra make up so as she would look good on the night.

All over Glasgow, the 3,000 Led Zeppelin ticket holders must have been doing that sort of thing – buying make up, smartening up their flares, trying on new T-shirts – so as they would look good on the night. Led Zeppelin was only going to happen once. It was important to get it right.

forty-five

I ALTERED MY JEANS WITH INFINITE CARE. I cut the outside seam up to the knee, carefully picking out the threads without damaging the material. I measured out a triangular piece of cloth with my school protractor and ruler and cut it to shape. I threaded the needle, doubling the cotton for extra strength as Suzy had demonstrated, pinned the material in place and got to work.

It was difficult forcing the needle through the thick seamed edge of the denim. Suzy had used a thimble. I didn't have a thimble so I forced each troublesome stitch through with a cassette of Uriah Heep's first album, *Very 'Eavy Very 'Umble*.

Uriah Heep is a character in *David Copperfield* by Charles Dickens. I had not read it at that time. When I got round to it, twenty or so years later, I enjoyed it, but I thought that Dickens gave Uriah quite a hard time; I could sympathise with the poor man's aspirations.

'When is it my turn to get the fabulous woman?' thinks Uriah Heep, more or less. But Dickens never lets him get the fabulous woman. Instead, he sends him to prison.

I sewed late into the night and carried on the next day. I was keen for this project to succeed. For one thing, I really needed something good to wear to see Led Zeppelin. For another, I was troubled to have found Greg at Suzy's house. It was highly significant that he hadn't phoned me before visiting her. He was edging ahead of me in getting close to Suzy. Suzy's relationship with Zed was now so unpredictable that there was no telling when she might need some emergency comforting. If Greg turned up with a much better pair of jeans than me, it would be one more thing in his favour.

For a first attempt at clothes alteration, it succeeded quite well. Inside, the fabric was a mass of poorly finished and uneven stitching, but on the outside they looked fine. I put them on and looked in the mirror. The new flares flopped around my ankles. I looked at Jimmy Page on the wall. Quite a similar effect. I was satisfied. I'd made them and they were good.

I went round to show Suzy. Zed was there and I somehow lost my enthusiasm and pretended I'd just gone round there for a visit, but Suzy noticed my jeans and said they looked great. She was enthusiastic. Her feline features lit up with pleasure. Suzy could really make you feel like you'd done something worthwhile.

Greg's trousers were also a success. He claimed to have done all the work himself but I suspected that his sister had helped him. I treacherously hinted at this to Suzy, which was the first time I'd ever put Greg down in any way.

Suzy and Zed didn't seem to be making much eye contact which probably meant they had been arguing again. I was always trying to pick up signals about the state of their relationship. I scanned their faces for signs of dissatisfaction as eagerly as I scanned the sky for the Monstrous Hordes of Xotha.

forty-six

SUZY HAD TWO NEW CHEESECLOTH SHIRTS, one yellow and one white.

"Which one do you like best?"

"White," I replied.

"Yellow," said Greg.

We eyed each other suspiciously.

"I think I like the yellow better," said Suzy.

Another crushing victory to Greg.

Suzy was annoyed because Zed had been due to take her out the night before but had failed to show up. He hadn't phoned. Suzy wasn't the type of girl to put up with that sort of behaviour.

Zed seemed to be becoming more and more inconsiderate. If he had been there, he probably wouldn't have cared about which cheesecloth shirt Suzy wore. Suzy asked us what we thought she should do about Zed. Greg and I were uncomfortable about this. Zed was our hero. We could never say anything bad about him. On the other hand, we lusted after Suzy. I felt unqualified to cope with the moral dilemma.

"Leave him," Greg blurted out suddenly. "You'd be better off finding a new boyfriend."

"That's right," I said, leaping in quickly. "You should leave him."

"Oh," said Suzy, and went quiet for a while. She didn't say anything more about the subject, and we got back to comparing the new shirts.

I walked through the streets with Greg. We didn't speak because we were ashamed of our treachery towards Zed. The rain beat down and the wind howled. It reminded me of our school production of *Macbeth*.

Zed was in the park, alone, slumped against the furthest wall, drunk. The rain made his long curly hair lie flat over his shoulders. As we approached he raised a bottle and shouted a greeting. The wine was cheap and rancid. I had rarely tasted anything so unpleasant. We told him Suzy was wondering where he was, but he didn't seem interested. He was too full of alcohol and Led Zeppelin to care about his girlfriend.

He wasn't being much of a boyfriend to Suzy. Maybe the advice we gave her wasn't really so bad. But it still seemed treacherous. I felt terrible about it.

The next day while we were walking to school, Greg wondered how it could be that two people could be in love with each other and yet not seem to like each other very much. I couldn't come up with an explanation. It didn't seem to make sense.

"And then there are Phil and Cherry," said Greg. "They like each other. But they'll never be in love, even though Phil wants it."

We were still laughing about Phil's hopeless passion for Cherry. But as our own hopeless passion grew, we weren't laughing so much.

forty-seven

AS A WARM UP FOR THE 1972 TOUR, Led Zeppelin had played some gigs in Sweden. Their first ever gigs had also been in Sweden, in 1969, when they were still called the New Yardbirds. The Yardbirds were the band that Jimmy Page was in before Led Zeppelin.

Page was a skilful guitarist from a young age. Before he joined the Yardbirds he was a session musician and much in demand by producers. John Paul Jones, Led Zeppelin's bass guitarist and keyboard player, was also a session musician. They were already very good at making other people's music before they started making their own

Although Led Zeppelin's two nights in Glasgow would be only the third and fourth gigs of their tour, I wasn't worried that they might not have warmed up properly. Earlier in the year, the band had toured America and Japan. Anyway, would the mighty Led Zeppelin really need to warm up? I doubted it.

I sat in class and imagined the powerful Zeppelin flying slowly northwards to Scotland. When teachers asked me questions about maths or English, I stared blankly back at them, my head too full of Led Zeppelin songs to reply. I had a partner in physics with whom I was meant to be studying acceleration. We did this by running a little trolley down a slope. The trolley was connected to a spool of ticker tape and a small machine punched holes in the ticker tape at regular time intervals. By studying how far apart the holes were you could measure the rate of acceleration.

'What are the readings?" she asked, and looked at me with annoyance as I hummed the riff for 'Whole Lotta Love'.

"Stop singing that. You've been singing that all week."

I was ruining the project. I didn't care. Led Zeppelin's imminent arrival made me too wild to concentrate on a physics project. I wouldn't have been any good at it anyway. Acceleration seemed to be measured in metres per second per second, and I never understood exactly what that meant.

My partner in physics was called Flo. Despite her frustration at my endless versions of 'Whole Lotta Love', she herself went to see Led Zeppelin. She wore a white cheesecloth blouse, blue jeans, red platform shoes and she frizzed her long black hair specially for the occasion. Later, she went to university in Edinburgh to study biology. After she obtained her degree, she moved back to Glasgow and married the boy she had gone out with at school. He wasn't at the gig. He didn't like Led Zeppelin. He didn't like any music. I don't know what happened to them after that.

Flo knew Jenny, who worked in the flower shop. She told me that Jenny was working herself into a state of dementia over the flowers for the dressing room. They had to be good. It had to be the best flower display ever seen backstage at Green's Playhouse.

Jenny was not unrealistic. She did not expect that when Led Zeppelin walked in to the dressing room they were going to be overwhelmed by the beauty of the flower arrangements and ask her to go on tour with them. They might not even notice the flowers. But she wanted to do a good job anyway, because she was mad about Led Zeppelin.

Suzy wasn't in my physics classes. In the third and fourth years we were in the same class for some subjects and different classes for others. I never liked any of the classes that she wasn't in. Flo told me it was heavily rumoured among the girls that Suzy and Zed had broken up. Suzy had told Zed she never wanted to see him again and this time she meant it. The trolley rolled down the slope and I let it crash to the floor. There were three days to the gig, and Suzy was now in need of comforting.

Later, Greg and I felt guilty again. We had advised Suzy to leave Zed. The thought of Suzy in need of comfort banished our guilt. I asked Greg what he was doing that night.

"Nothing," he replied. "I'll probably just stay in."

forty-eight

THE HUGE ZEPPELIN FLEW TOWARDS GLASGOW. Inside were Jimi Hendrix, Janis Joplin, Sonny Boy Williamson and Hank Williams, all come out of their celestial homes to see Led Zeppelin.

They played cards and drank and talked about old times. Sonny Boy Williamson played a tune on his harmonica, the same harmonica he'd taken with him in a box car all the way from Tennessee to a nightclub in Chicago.

They talked about Bryan Jones, who was dead, and Elvis, who was still alive.

"So what happened to you?" asked Sonny.

"I overdosed in '70," said Janis Joplin.

"Tough break."

Janis shrugged.

"It was bound to happen. Near the end, I was getting careless."

Greg and I looked up in the sky to see if the Zeppelin was in sight yet. Soon we would have to fly up on our dragons and protect it from the Monstrous Hordes of Xotha. Rock stars, alive or dead, didn't normally figure in the sword and sorcery world of the Monstrous Hordes of Xotha and their evil leader Kuthimas, but times were strange. With the imminent arrival of Led Zeppelin, everything seemed to be coming together in a confusing fashion.

Kuthimas was so malevolent he may well have tried to spoil the gig. His dragons might have attacked the Zeppelin. It was up to us to protect it.

forty-nine

SUZY STUCK TO HER DECISION about breaking up with Zed and told him never to contact her again. So then Zed was much nicer to her, and called her on the phone to be friendly and conciliatory. Just because Zed was the coolest boy in school, it didn't make him particularly good at relationships. I didn't realise that at the time. I assumed he was good at everything.

Zed's situation at home worsened. His parents discovered that he was no longer going to school, but was instead spending his days either in the house or visiting his student friends in Byers Road.

Suzy told me that Zed's father had forbidden him to go and see Led Zeppelin. Apparently, he had suddenly decided that they were a bad influence on his son. Somehow that made sense in my world of the time. When children became too troublesome, parents would take revenge.

Zed had no intention of not going to the gig, but his father told him that if he did then he would no longer be welcome in the house.

"What's Zed going to do?"

Suzy didn't know. Zed was old enough to leave school and get a job, but it was hardly possible for him to organise an income and a place to live in the next two days.

I asked Suzy if Zed was still her boyfriend.

"Of course," she replied.

She sounded annoyed that I could ask such a thing, even though only a day before she had sworn they would never get back together.

"Perhaps Zed and I should get married," she mused.

That evening Greg and I were depressed. We didn't

like it that Zed was in such trouble. Furthermore, Suzy had mentioned the word 'married'.

"Why would anyone want to get married so young?"

Many people I knew at school were settled down and well on the way to middle age by the time they were twenty-two. Foolish behaviour. Everyone should tour the world and see as many Led Zeppelin gigs as possible.

fifty

AT SCHOOL THERE WAS A SMALL LIBRARY which was never open when you wanted it to be. You couldn't sit in there at lunch-time if it was cold and wet outside. You couldn't go and look up anything on your own, though occasionally the whole class would be dragged along to research into some project or other.

Projects bored me. I never completed them, never did anything beyond put my name on the outside of a note pad. That seemed like quite enough, although it did mean I was obliged to offer up silent prayers in class that the teacher did not ask me to read a chapter out loud.

I had a horror of reading out loud in those days. Fortunately, I have now got over this. These days I am quite happy to stand up in front of an audience and read, even wearing an afghan coat if I feel like it.

While the rest of the class busied themselves in their inquiries into Egyptian farming, Scottish wool production, or the state of trade on the River Danube, I stared into space and thought about Led Zeppelin.

Cherry wandered up to me. She was wearing a badge that said Library Monitor.

"Look," she declaimed in a voice loud enough to be heard in the playground outside. "I've found a book of Celtic myths. It's got fairies and dragons. Do you want to look at it?"

I cringed and tried to shut her up, but I was too late. Bassy leapt over and grabbed the book. He laughed, louder than was permitted in the library, and the teacher frowned at him.

"You spastic!" he said, in a stage whisper that everyone could hear, and afterwards he told the class what a homosexual I was turning out to be. He never let me forget that occasion, and when he had nothing better to do, would torment me as the boy who looked at pictures of fairies, one of the severest crimes imaginable.

After school I confronted Cherry.

"Are you mad?" I demanded.

"What's the matter?"

"What's the matter? Why did you have to start waving a book of fairies around? Now everyone's laughing at me."

"There were dragons too," said Cherry. "I thought you'd want to see them."

That was too stupid for words. I swore at her then stormed off, furious.

"I think I might be able to fix Zed's robot," called Cherry.

I would have turned and abused her again but I had just spotted Bassy approaching, and I couldn't take any more of him today.

Bassy wanted to be a professional footballer but he was never good enough. He did end up as quite a successful businessman though, and owns two garages in Glasgow, and another in Motherwell, and a laundry in Paisley.

It had been a bad day at school. At lunch-time Suzy had gone off for a private conversation with Greg. That was very worrying. Already I could see that he was becoming closer to her. And yesterday I'd thought he was less keen than usual on hunting out the Monstrous Hordes of Xotha.

I trudged home on my own. Led Zeppelin was two days away. I looked at the posters on my walls and again wished that I was older, that I was seeing Led Zeppelin in Vancouver or New York or London instead of being stuck in school in Glasgow.

fifty-one

THAT EVENING I CALLED GREG. His mother answered the phone. Greg wasn't home and she didn't know where he was. I called Suzy. She wasn't home either. I wondered if they had gone off somewhere together. I considered phoning Zed but decided against it. I rarely called him, fearing that he might not like it.

I wandered out into the street outside where spots of rain were drifting through the white light of the street lamps. I wrapped my greatcoat around me and put on my new shades. I liked them. I couldn't see very much but I thought they were a very cool addition.

It was freezing, so I hurried along the street on my own, not going anywhere, just walking to warm myself up. The gig was fast approaching but, oddly, the overwhelming excitement seemed to have ebbed. I was depressed about Suzy. I would never get anywhere with her. We would never have any sort of relationship. Here she was, on her own for a few days and already she was off enjoying herself with Greg.

At the end of the street there was some sort of power generator, guarded by a fence with a warning sign from the electricity board to keep off. I leant against the fence, sheltering from the wind, and looked up at the sky. There was nothing there: no Zeppelins, no fabulous beasts, no visitors from Atlantis.

I shivered, and realised with disgust that Atlantis didn't exist. It wouldn't rise from the waves when Led Zeppelin played in Glasgow. Nothing would happen except Suzy and Greg would probably be kissing each other in the row in front of me and I'd get thrown out of the auditorium for being the only depressed person in the audience.

"Hello," said Cherry, appearing beside me.

I gave her a hostile glare.

"I'm sorry I embarrassed you about the fairy book," she said, and she did look very sorry.

I shrugged. "It's okay."

"Why are you standing here?"

I shrugged again.

"Are you depressed about Suzy?" asked Cherry.

"Why do you say that?"

"It's obvious," replied Cherry, and I realised that of course it was. Probably everybody knew. Another humiliation.

I was desperate for someone to listen to my problems. So I told her that yes, I was very unhappy about Suzy. Cherry listened to this for a long time, laying her violin case carefully on a dry patch of ground.

"I hate the violin," she said.

"Why do you play it?"

"My parents make me."

I admired her honesty. I told her more about Suzy.

fifty-two

I'M IN THE SUPERMARKET WITH MANX.

"So you started bleating about Suzy to Cherry?"

"Of course. Why not?"

"No reason I suppose," says Manx. "Though you might say you haven't moved on much in the last twenty-six years. You still complain to me about women you love that don't love you back."

"Thank you for reminding me."

I pick up a peach and squeeze it to see if it's ripe. It gives under the pressure of my fingers. I put it back on the shelf. I'm not buying a squashed peach.

"I'm sure I've moved on in some areas."

We are unexpectedly caught up in quite a serious lettuce incident. Manx is wheeling her baby chair round the corner of the vegetable display when she has to break sharply to avoid ramming a woman who has suddenly changed direction towards the potatoes. Taken by surprise, I crash into Manx and she nudges a tray of lettuces, bringing it tumbling onto the floor.

Each green vegetable, wrapped up securely in cling film, bounces and rolls as it hits the floor. In no time there are lettuces everywhere.

"It's a vegetable disaster," I cry.

We look at the floor, awash with lettuce, but we don't make any attempt to pick them up. We make for the check-out, undaunted.

"You see," I tell Manx, "we are making progress in life. At one time a big lettuce incident like that would have had a very bad effect on us. The assistants would have intimidated us and we'd probably have had to run out of the shop, humiliated. Now, who cares? Let the shop assistants stare. We can take it."

We pay for our goods and depart. Manx is coming to my house. We are going to start the judging process.

"Have you read any of the books yet?"

"No. They all look too dull. If I had to give a prize for the dullest book, I could do it right away.

fifty-three

WHEN I'D FINALLY OPENED THE BOX, I'd found to my surprise that it wasn't all books. Some of it was manuscripts. Bits of paper waiting to be turned into books. This was a competition for first novels, but some of the novels weren't published yet.

"This makes it harder, Manx. The manuscripts are quite unwieldy. Also, I was depending on reading the blurbs on the back of the books to get me off to some sort of start, but the manuscripts don't have blurbs."

"There's some poetry here."

"I know. And I swear no one mentioned anything about poetry. Why would anyone think that I was competent to judge poetry?"

"It is strange," agrees Manx. "But judging a book of poems can't be as difficult as judging a novel. No need to read much, just glance at a few verses and get a rough idea of what's going on."

Manx says she will work out a judging system. She has academic training. I take the baby with me to the kitchen to make some tea.

"How about point scores from one to five in various categories?" suggests Manx, when I return with the tray.

"What categories?"

"The cover, the blurb if available, the first page, the author's financial statement, the author's photograph, and the author's statement of intent. That way you can make an assessment without having to read any of the books."

This sounds impressive.

"Excellent. If I turn up on judging day with lots of tables and figures no one can say I haven't been taking things seriously."

We sort out the books and manuscripts into two piles, one for Manx and one for me.

"Can we have an emergency category for any author who's really attractive that I might want to sleep with?" I ask Manx.

"Do you think that giving her the prize would be a help?"

"It couldn't do any harm."

"Okay. If there's anyone that it looks like you might want to sleep with, we'll award an extra ten points."

All the authors' financial statements are bad. Most of them include details of signing on for social security. But to be honest, I don't even know why the financial statements are here. As far as I know, I'm meant to be judging the books on merit alone. Might the organisers have mentioned something about giving the prize to someone who needed money most? I can't remember. I wasn't paying attention.

I notice that Manx is looking distracted.

"Bored with it?"

"I was thinking about my so-called friend Jean. You know she's been talking about me behind my back? She's always putting me down."

Manx tells me that this friend has been in competition with her from the moment they both became pregnant.

I can understand this. People are always in competition about weird things, things that don't matter to anyone else. Book competitions. Baby competitions. At school I was always trying to grow my hair longer than Greg.

After Greg left school, he went to work in a shipping office and later moved into the oil business. He never played in a band. I haven't been in contact with him for years now, but I know that he moved to Sweden and is a high-up executive in an oil firm. He will undoubtedly have a great deal more money than me.

"But he won't be able to stay up all night watching television," I say.

We get back to judging. Manx is now gloomy about her friend Jean talking about her behind her back. I wish I could cheer her up.

fifty-four

WE'RE WALKING BACK TOWARDS MANX'S FLAT.

"Manx, I have a new plan. I've decided not to get old. In fact, more than that, I have decided to be fourteen again."

"And how are you going to defy the laws of space and time?"

"I'll do it by going to see Led Zeppelin every night. Getting that bootleg of the gig has really changed my life. I figure that every evening I could get ready like I was going to the gig in 1972 – you know, light some incense, put on my Led Zeppelin T-shirt and some flared jeans. Do you think buying a long wig would be going too far? Maybe you're right. But anyway, I'll drink some beer, walk around the streets for a while like I'm going to the venue, and then come home and put on the live tape really loud and pretend I'm at Green's Playhouse. It'll be great."

"You've never actually been to the Maudsley, have you?" asks Manx.

The Maudsley is a psychiatric hospital in Camberwell. It's quite a well-known place. The 35 bus goes there from Brixton.

"No. Well yes, but only to visit people."

I tell Manx she can mock all she wants. I'm going to spend the rest of my life pretending it's 1972 and I'm watching Led Zeppelin.

"What makes it better is that I now have seven episodes of *Man About the House* on video. *Man About the House* was a big favourite with me and Greg. It was the best TV show. We were both very attracted to Sally Thomsett. She had blonde hair like Suzy. I never actually saw her in a Led Zeppelin T-shirt, but she did have an afghan coat and really great platform clogs. I can watch a different episode every night of the week then listen to my Zeppelin bootleg."

"And while it's playing, I can turn out the lights and put on my video of *The Song Remains the Same,* the Led Zeppelin film. So it will be just like I'm watching them on stage. But I'll turn the sound down on the TV and play the live tape because the Glasgow show was much better than the one they recorded for the film. Why do you think that is?"

It has always puzzled me that Led Zeppelin, with a wealth of fine performances all over the world, many of them recorded, chose to use a not very good one for their official film. But it will do for some visuals anyway.

"Isn't it a great idea? I'll still have plenty of time in the day to write books and wash the dishes and stuff. Do you want to come over and join me?"

Manx declines. She has to make a new piece of animation about a tree blowing in the wind and then turning into a dragon.

"It's all foolish," I tell her. "Moving forward in life won't bring you happiness. Look at Greg. He's an executive for an oil company, somewhere in Scandinavia. How miserable can your life get? I bet he thinks about Jimmy Page and Sally Thomsett every day."

"Of course he doesn't. He'll be too busy being an executive."

"Well, that just proves my point. His life is such a shambles that he doesn't even have time to think about Led Zeppelin any more."

"What happened to Zed after he left school?" asks Manx.

"I don't think Zed liked *Man About the House* as much as Greg and me. It wasn't really cool enough. Sitcoms were kind of below Zed's notice. I'm too hot. The sun's giving me a headache. Can we go into a shop? I need to get out of the sun."

fifty-five

ZED MOVED IN WITH SOME STUDENT FRIENDS in town. His mother was very unhappy about this but his father wouldn't have him back in the house. I worried about him, though Suzy assured me that he was well enough.

I'd have liked to discuss it with Greg but I was getting on less well with him. As Suzy's relationship with Zed lurched from one crisis to another, we'd managed to convince ourselves that she was going to be picking up a new boyfriend any day now, and we were the only candidates in view. Without ever voicing it, we became suspicious of each other. It occurred to me that, as Greg and I had not hesitated to criticise Zed to Suzy,

Greg might now be criticising me. He had once again visited Suzy without telling me, even though he actually had to walk past my house to get there. A line from Led Zeppelin came to me, about wanting to be some girl's backdoor man. I thought about Greg as Suzy's backdoor man, sneaking past my house to visit her in private. Of course, at the time I didn't know that backdoor man was a slang way of referring to anal intercourse. Probably when I was fifteen I didn't know that there was such a thing. I was very ignorant about sex when I was young. I was too busy looking for dragon armies in the sky. I rescued princesses, but I never slept with them afterwards, just moved on to the next princess.

"You shouldn't fall out with Greg over Suzy," said Cherry. "Friendships are important."

I scowled at her. Just because Cherry was a good person for talking to about Suzy didn't mean I wanted loads of ridiculous advice from her. I simply wanted her to listen, and hopefully, put in a good word for me with Suzy. And she still couldn't join the Dragon Army.

"It's out of the question," I told her. "Girls can't be in the Dragon Army."

"I've drawn a picture of you on a dragon," she said.

She brought out a piece of paper from her bag. It showed me riding on a dragon. I had a sword in my hand and my hair was streaming behind me in the wind. It was a good picture.

"I didn't know you could draw."

"Can I be in the Dragon Army now?"

I shook my head. It was only for me and Greg. If Greg deserted I'd run it myself. That wasn't ideal but it would have to do.

"Do you know Phil is attracted to you?" I asked her.

Cherry did. She told me she liked Phil, and he was a

good partner for playing music with, but she wasn't attracted to him.

"I don't think of him that way."

fifty-six

I'M GETTING READY FOR THE GIG. I've got a pair of jeans with flared insets, a cheap pair of baseball boots and a blue tie-dyed T-shirt, same as always. I'd like to wear something special but I don't have anything special. I look in the mirror. My skin is pure, unscarred, no wrinkles. It makes me look younger than fifteen. My hair is very long, way past my shoulders, and very blond. I could be a Viking invader from the land of the ice and snow, except I'm too puny to carry a sword.

I have a pair of dark glasses. I put them on, and put on my greatcoat over my T-shirt. The ill-fitting coat won't keep me warm outside but I don't want to be wearing anything else. I can't be messing around with jackets at the gig and no one wears jerseys. I look in the mirror. I'm not completely satisfied but it will have to do.

I'm meeting Greg at the gig. It's less of an arrangement than it might have been. Normally we'd have met beforehand, close to an off-licence, prior to buying alcohol, but the stress of competing for Suzy is affecting everything about our friendship.

Neither of us are travelling to the gig with Suzy. She got fed up with us phoning her all the time and decided to go there with Cherry instead. Cherry's father is giving them a lift into town. I can't travel with them because Cherry's parents are still annoyed with me over the theft of the diary, even though Cherry has forgiven me.

The thought of Suzy with Cherry makes me nervous. I'd hate it if Cherry hinted to Suzy that I was in love with her. On the other hand, I hope she hints to Suzy that I am in love with her.

I put my ticket in my pocket and pray that I won't lose it before I get there. I know that I'm nervous and incompetent enough to do that. My hands are damp with perspiration and I can feel myself twitching. I look at the Led Zeppelin posters on the wall and I tell the band that I'll be seeing them soon. I look Robert Plant right in the eye. He looks back at me. I run my hand over the posters, making sure to touch all four band members, and then I run out of the house.

There's only one bus into the centre of town from here, the 172. It is bitterly cold at the bus stop. A fierce December wind is whipping though the streets. It's dark already. In winter the daylight seems to last for no time at all; I walk to school and back in darkness. I'm freezing. The wind is seeking out the open seams in my greatcoat, working its way through the ripped lining and chilling me through my T-shirt.

Unexpectedly, Greg appears at the bus stop.

"I thought you were taking the early bus?"

"Trouble with the parents," he grunts.

We look at each other awkwardly. Rain starts to stream from the sky and we move under the bus shelter. We're close together. I can feel Greg in my space. I get a weird urge to hug him. I resist the urge, though it's powerful. To take my mind off it, I start marching up and down humming the riff from 'Communication Breakdown'. Greg joins in and we forget our awkwardness and start babbling with uncontrollable excitement about Led Zeppelin.

"What if they don't come?" says Greg, suddenly becoming as anxious as me.

Out of the darkness Suzy and Cherry appear, their coats pulled tightly round their thin schoolgirl bodies. Suzy is wearing her afghan and seems far too exotic and beautiful for this dull corner of Glasgow. Her hair is blonder than ever, blonde enough to shine through the gloom, brighter than the streetlights. Her eyes are made up in subtle shades of grey and blue, her eyelids are dark with kohl and her eyelashes curl delicately under her mascara. Greg and I gaze at her with wonder.

Cherry looks the same as she always does, and is wearing a particularly offensive overcoat that looks like it might be her father's. At least she's not wearing her school blazer.

"I thought you were getting a lift into town?"

"Trouble with the parents," says Cherry.

Now I get a powerful urge to kiss Suzy. I repress it by launching into the riff for 'Whole Lotta Love'.

Da-da da-da DA da-da da-da

For the first and only time Suzy joins in. She doesn't normally sing guitar riffs. Greg and Cherry also join in and the four of us stand in the wind and the rain at the bus stop singing the world famous riff to 'Whole Lotta Love'.

Da-da da-da DA da-da da-da
Da-da da-da DA da-da da-da

When it comes to the psychedelic part in the middle of the song, we make weird noises that fly away on the wind. The bus arrives and we leap aboard.

"Led Zeppelin," says Cherry, and the four of us scream, so the bus conductor frowns at us in disapproval.

fifty-seven

WE'RE NOT CERTAIN WHERE ZED WILL BE. On a night like this he will have better company than us. As we arrive at the bus station in Buchanan Street we rush off, impatiently barging past older people who have come into town to do whatever it is older people do. Dull things, I imagine.

Suzy, who looks the oldest, collects money from us all and disappears into an off-licence while we hang back in the shadows. Beside us on the pavement, some other youths wait for the same reason. We're close to the venue and the streets are full of Led Zeppelin fans on their way to the gig, some hugging their coats to keep out the cold and some smiling and waving their arms in excitement, oblivious to the weather.

Suzy is gone a long time. We become anxious in case she has been refused service, but eventually she appears with a carrier bag clutched to her chest. We disappear down an alleyway to quickly drink our beer and pour vodka into bottles of orange juice which we can take in with us.

No one at the venue can have been fooled by streams of underage people coming in with bottles of allegedly non-alcoholic coke or orange juice. I suppose they didn't care. It never occurred to anyone not to try to drink at the earliest possible opportunity.

I raise my eyes and I can see all sorts of things flying over the dark strip of sky above the alley. Zeppelins and fabulous beasts lurk behind the clouds. Greg drinks faster than me, and more. So does Suzy. Cherry says that she has never drunk alcohol before. Normally we'd mock her mercilessly for this, but now there are more important things to think about.

I'm almost concentrating totally on Led Zeppelin but it still causes me a twinge of pain that when we emerge from the alleyway Greg is walking beside Suzy and I'm stuck with Cherry.

We practically crash into Zed who is walking up to the gig with a grin on his face, his afghan coat flapping in the wind and a can of Special Brew in his hand. He's with a large group of friends but he greets us cheerfully anyway, raising his can in salute.

He has a girl on his arm. I think her name is Fiona. She's older than Suzy, and nearly as pretty. I've met her before, at a student party Zed took us to. This party was a precious memory, the first real grown-up social gathering I'd ever been to. I enjoyed it, though I sat the whole night in a corner and never spoke to anyone.

"You should've called me," says Zed to Greg and me, though he only nods to Suzy.

"Hello Zed," says Cherry, with too much enthusiasm.

Zed puts his arm round her, puts his face close to her cheek and says it's good to see her. He kisses her lightly.

I'm shocked. He doesn't seem to care that he's with friends from the university, or that they can see him with his arm round a stupid little nerdy girl with terrible red hair and horrible clothes.

Suzy's face is dark and angry. I cunningly slip my hand into hers in a comforting manner. All around the venue people are selling posters and shouting for tickets, to buy or to sell. We join the crush of bodies at the entrance to Green's Playhouse, old Scottish cinema, one time music hall, now home for the night to the greatest rock and roll event in the history of the world.

fifty-eight

"I COULDN'T UNDERSTAND WHY ZED KISSED CHERRY," I tell Manx. "I thought at the time he was trying to make Suzy jealous, but there were other women around he could have kissed instead. Fiona on his arm was already more than enough to make Suzy jealous. It just seemed weird that he'd show affection to Cherry."

"Although Zed and Suzy walked in about ten feet apart, you could still feel the energy between them. They really had a powerful thing going on. Some unbreakable attraction. Even when they weren't speaking to each other it never went away. I don't think that ever happened to me. Did it ever happen to you?"

"I thought so once," says Manx. "But it disappeared after a while."

We stare at the TV for a while. We're watching a cartoon.

"Zed was so magnetic. Maybe he would have produced that sort of effect in any relationship. You know I told you I wanted to hug Greg at the bus stop? And kiss Suzy? That was nothing compared to what I felt about Zed. If people at school had known what I felt about Zed, I'd have been lynched."

Probably I wasn't the only boy at school who felt attracted to Zed. Like practically everything else, I didn't realise this at the time.

I still think about Zed a lot. And Led Zeppelin. They dominated my life from 1971 to 1976. Then the Sex Pistols instigated punk rock. Led Zeppelin suddenly looked very old-fashioned. I was living in London and still feeling young enough for teenage rebellion. I cut my hair, dyed it red, put a safety-pin through my cheek, had treatment at St Thomas's Hospital for the subsequent serious infection, and had fun.

If Led Zeppelin looked old-fashioned in 1977, other bands looked a lot worse. I kept my Led Zeppelin records but I got rid of everything else. I sold records by Emerson Lake and Palmer, Man, Iron Butterfly, Black Sabbath, Deep Purple, David Bowie, the Groundhogs, Blue Cheer, Hawkwind, Mott the Hoople and many others.

That was a mistake. Never get rid of your records. You'll want them again some day, if only to look at the covers. Hawkwind's *Space Ritual* had a spectacular cover. It folded out into a giant chart, six times the size of the album. It had pictures, poems, snatches of philosophy and plenty else besides. It even gave the date of the sinking of Atlantis, 9850 BC.

Modern scientists put the date slightly earlier, at 1040 BC. Well, maybe not scientists exactly.

Nowadays, I listen to Led Zeppelin a lot. They have stood the test of time, oh yes.

"What happened to Zed after school?" asks Manx.

"It was strange that he kissed Cherry," I reply. "I don't like this cartoon. Let's watch *Buffy* videos."

fifty-nine

INSIDE GREEN'S PLAYHOUSE there are no decorations, no banners, no incense burning, nothing to indicate that anything special is about to happen. There's a red curtain in front of the stage and, except for the metal security fence at the front, we might all be here to see a film.

Even before the lights go down the hall is dim and poorly lit. The carpet is sticky underfoot. My ticket is for row H, eight rows from the front, over to the right of the stage. The seats are dark red, once plush but now tired and sagging. I file down the aisle and make my way along, too excited to wait for Greg or Suzy or Cherry. They struggle after me, squeezing past bodies in the confused throng of fans.

Zed and his friends are in the row behind us. As soon as the band arrive, I know Zed will leap to the front with one mighty bound. He catches my eye and raises his bottle of coke to me in a salute.

Soon after I take my seat, the curtain is drawn back revealing keyboards, drums and guitars on stands. There's also a long upright metal pole which I take to be the theremin, the strange instrument which Robert Plant uses to make weird electronic noises.

Cherry is on my left. She's holding her glasses in her hand. She'll need them to see the gig properly, but she doesn't want to put them on before the lights go down. Suzy is on my right and beyond her is Greg. I turn to Greg and we look at each other with great excitement because now we've actually seen the instruments that Led Zeppelin will play.

"Isn't there a support act?" asks Cherry.

"Led Zeppelin don't have support acts any more. It's just them. That's Jimmy Page's guitar right there on the stage. It's a Gibson SG."

Cherry looks at me like I'm a man who knows a lot about Led Zeppelin. I'm pleased. Really, I have no idea what sort of guitar it is.

Around us there is a lot of long hair, a lot of denim and a great aroma of patchouli oil. There are some people I know from school and others I recognise from gigs. I turn round to Suzy to point out her cousin, but Suzy has her back to me. She's leaning over towards Greg. I can feel that they're developing a bond. I don't like it. Zed taps me on the shoulder. He puts his arm round my neck and, as he draws my face close to his, I can smell the alcohol on his breath. He puts his mouth to my ear and says, just loud enough for me to hear over the noise of the crowd, "Stop worrying about Suzy. Suzy is an idiot."

I'm puzzled, but his face is only inches from mine and I can't interpret his expression.

"She's you're girlfriend."

"I got stuck with it. My misfortune."

He grins. "You should go out with Cherry. Much better woman."

No one has ever called Cherry a woman. Is Zed mocking me? He's never mocked me before. I laugh, trying to share a joke though I'm not sure what the joke is. Fiona, who is sitting beside Zed, leans over and puts her arm round him, dragging him closer.

Suzy is in close conversation with Greg, and her face is like thunder. Either she heard what Zed said to me or she's seen Fiona trying to kiss him. Cherry is staring straight in front of her, eyes shining with excitement. She's taken off her coat and her Led Zeppelin T-shirt is the newest and cleanest T-shirt in the whole of Green's Playhouse. She didn't even know enough to wear it in first, to make it look older.

A roadie with extremely long hair walks onto the stage and makes some adjustment to an amplifier. At the sight of this, the crowd roar and I banish everything from my mind except Led Zeppelin.

sixty

NOW I'VE COME TO THE START OF THE GIG. So the next fifteen chapters or so are pretty much just me dancing around in Green's Playhouse, listening to Led Zeppelin and having a fabulous time. But read on. For one thing, I get my first proper kiss. For another, the gig will be over before you know it and then you'll be back in the real world, and how much fun is that?

Led Zeppelin walk on stage. I get a very strange feeling in my chest before I'm carried off to a place where I am not troubled by worldly cares.

Greg tugs at my sleeve.

"Atlantis has risen from the waves," he yells, and I grin at him.

The band strolls out and nods to the audience. We immediately make as much noise as it is possible for 3,000 people to make, cheering, whistling, clapping, stamping, just screaming in pleasure at the sight of Robert Plant, Jimmy Page, John Paul Jones and John Bonham. There are a few electronic jarrings as Jimmy Page and John Paul Jones get their guitars in place, a brief crackle from the speakers, then John Bonham starts up with the introduction from 'Rock and Roll'. The crowd is now making so much noise that the end of the drum intro is lost under the volume, and the music doesn't emerge till Jimmy Page starts up the guitar riff.

At this moment, some ten seconds or so after the start of the gig, most of the audience abandons their seats and stampedes towards the front. Zed puts his hands on my shoulders, vaults over me and then runs over the heads of the people in front to throw himself against the wall of bouncers at the foot of the stage. I try to follow but I'm caught up and trampled in the rush. A hand reaches down and hauls me to my feet. It's Cherry, displaying a surprising amount of strength. She drags me after her into the aisle and then down towards the front.

It's astonishing the way she scythes her way through. Whether it's the effects of the band or the alcohol, Cherry mows her way onwards, pulling me in her wake till all that stands between us and Led Zeppelin is a single line of gyrating fans and a thin metal crash barrier.

The bouncers, defeated by our furious enthusiasm, retreat behind the barrier and stare out in a hostile manner, knowing that nothing they can do will get us back in our seats. I raise my hands above my head and start clapping in time with the beat, and screaming, not in time with anything. Everyone is screaming. Glasgow voices, quite harsh, not melodious like the voices of Scots from the Highlands.

Robert Plant is singing, Jimmy Page's guitar punctuates every line, just like on the record. Here they are, playing it right in front of us, maybe twenty feet away from where I'm standing with my arms in the air, still screaming.

The audience sings along. We know all the lyrics, and the guitar lines, and the drum breaks. We also know that for the next few hours there is really nothing to worry about.

Robert Plant gets the words wrong in the second verse but it's okay, he just keeps going. He exchanges a grin with Jimmy Page. I love them even more, if that's possible. If I'd been able to think anything very coherent at this moment, I'd be thinking that if I had to die right after the gig, it would be okay. After all, I'd have seen Led Zeppelin play.

What would life be like without music? Unbearable. Music is a gift from God.

sixty-one

'ROCK AND ROLL' ENDS. The audience is still screaming, so that as the music stops the volume hardly decreases. I'm crushed right alongside Cherry and behind Zed. I crane my neck but I can't see any sign of Suzy or Greg.

Jimmy Page strums his guitar and goes quickly into an unfamiliar riff. Several times, I've had dull experiences at gigs when bands insisted on playing their new songs instead of the ones I wanted to hear, but I'm confident that Led Zeppelin will play my favourites. And I'm not worried about new songs. If Led Zeppelin play new songs they will be good. Possibly even monumental. There is no chance of Led Zeppelin turning up in Glasgow with a bunch of dull songs. Cosmic law forbids it.

Robert Plant starts to sing. I can't catch the words. Something about a lady having the love he needs. The vocal PA at the Playhouse was never very good. Sometimes you could barely hear the singer. However, Robert Plant is not a man to be defeated by a poor PA and after a quiet introduction the song springs into life. The crowd around me starts dancing up and down, and I dance up and down with them. It feels good.

Nearby, a young man who looks like a student with his very long hair and afghan waistcoat, climbs on top of the person in front of him and starts crawling over the shoulders and heads of the people in front before plunging down through their ranks. All around people are doing this sort of thing, practically surfing over the crowd. I've never seen this done before, and don't see it again for a long time afterwards. It's not like any other gig. Hysteria is in the air, and it feels good.

'Over the Hills and Far Away' ends to the sound of more yelling and screaming and shouting. Robert Plant speaks to the audience for the first time. His Midlands accent sounds soft and pleasant to me, and very English. It doesn't surprise me that he sounds like this, I've heard his voice on Zed's radio tapes.

"Our second night in Glasgow," he says, which brings more cheers.

"Our second time in four and a half years which seems a little overdue, I must admit," he continues.

We love him for mentioning Glasgow.

"We've only been here about thirty-six hours – maybe even twenty-four – and we've been in some trouble…"

This produces fantastic applause. Meanwhile, Jimmy Page is tuning his guitar in the background. John Paul Jones stands quietly with his bass, watching the audience. The aroma of patchouli oil wafts over me.

"This one's about a friend of ours, about nineteen years old and he's been in trouble… he couldn't take no more bitches…"

They crash into the riff of 'Out on the Tiles', always one of my Zeppelin favourites, though not one of their most famed numbers. Then, spectacularly, as the riff pauses, they launch instead into 'Black Dog'. This, of course, is the opening track on the fourth album, released only this year. I've already listened to it hundreds of times in my bedroom. Thousands of times. I know all the words because I sing them every morning when I'm delivering newspapers. I jump up and down and shake my head so my hair swirls around, and start singing along. It's wonderful. Nothing was ever so good.

sixty-two

WHEN LED ZEPPELIN PLAYED at Green's Playhouse it was the best feeling in the world. I will never feel that way again. No group of musicians can affect me that way now. I'm too old for it to happen. I regret this.

No doubt many people remember this same feeling.

"Of course, it might not relate to Led Zeppelin," I admit to Manx. "I wouldn't insist that the band that meant most to me must be the same one that meant most to everyone."

Manx tells me that when her step-brother went to see the legendary Kool Herc, the man who invented breakbeats, he was so overwhelmed he couldn't speak of anything else for weeks.

"And I know a woman who says that her life was transformed by going to see Nirvana," continues Manx. "She'd spent three months listening to their first CD for ten hours every day and when she finally got to see them she was so overwhelmed she gave up her job and started learning guitar."

It might be Elvis Presley, the Rolling Stones or Public Enemy. Maybe the night you heard Kemistry and Storm DJ was the best night you ever had. The Manic Street Preachers, the Smiths, the Sex Pistols, Todd Terry, Marilyn Manson or any number of people. The band who made life bearable when you were skulking in your bedroom with the rest of the world against you. At least one time in your life everything was perfect.

Led Zeppelin in Glasgow. Before it I was frustrated and after it I was disappointed. But when the band played, everything was right.

sixty-three

LED ZEPPELIN THUNDER THROUGH 'BLACK DOG'. Robert Plant throws back his head and wails, and the great juddering sound rolls off the stage, tossing us up and down like waves in a storm.

There's a point in this song where the music stops and Robert Plant sings on his own, 'Ah ah ah ah' before the riff crunches in again. When it comes to this point in the song, Plant sings the first few ahs then points the mike at the audience, and we howl back a chorus of ahs in perfect time, with great enthusiasm. Everyone is happy about this. Robert Plant shakes his long blond hair, which goes red as the stage lights wash over it. The lights here are simple, single colours that sweep across the stage, changing from red to blue to green. Even this simple display was more than enough to set off some wild hallucinations in the heads of young rock fans making their first experiments with LSD.

Jimmy Page extends the guitar solo and then makes the radical change of playing the riff an octave higher. We get to sing the ahs again, there's some extra guitar and then an abrupt ending that leaves the audience momentarily dazed with elation. When the applause starts it sounds like more noise than 3,000 people could make, it sounds like Hamden Stadium when Scotland have just scored a goal. It goes on and on. Robert Plant tries to introduce the next song and grins when his voice is completely drowned out by the extended howling. All four of the band look round at each other, smiling. They look happy at the reaction, even though they must be well used to this sort of thing.

Finally Plant gets to speak.

135

"We'd like to dedicate this next number to the Central Hotel."

This unexpected mention of a hotel in Glasgow produces another great wave of cheering. It's good to have Led Zeppelin mentioning a building in our city. We feel honoured.

They launch into 'Misty Mountain Hop'. We all clap along furiously till the riff changes and puts us out of tempo. Led Zeppelin were good at these time shifts. Despite the fact that their songs often sound pretty straight forward, there is quite a lot of time changing going on. They could get away with this because they were such great rock musicians.

What a band. "Fantastic," as someone bellows in my ear right next to me, and I grin at him, and get back to leaping up and down.

sixty-four

MORE PEOPLE ARE ARRIVING at the front all the time, trying to get closer to the band. Some newcomers squash their way in from the sides, forcing Cherry and me backwards. Cherry refuses to stand for this and elbows her way back through. I follow in her wake. I have to admire her determination. At this rate, she'll soon be invading the stage.

Zed is still right at the front. No amount of interlopers can move him. Greg and Suzy haven't made it this far forward. I risk a glance round and, though I can't be sure, I think I glimpse them holding hands as the band goes into 'Since I've Been Loving You', a slow blues.

I used to divide Led Zeppelin songs into three varieties: heavy rock, hippy/Celtic mysticism, and the blues. These were not inflexible categories, but it was a workable enough system.

Of the three types, my least favourite was the blues. I had no problem imagining myself rambling through the misty mountains with elves and hobbits at my side – I did it every morning on my paper round – but I found it harder to relate to the blues. Their blues songs, all about mean women and buying jewels for your baby, seem to belong to another world. Even in 1972 it seemed dated. No one thought that buying your baby diamonds and pearls was the best way to go about things. Women were now known to have intellects. They didn't even like being called baby any more.

None of this mattered to me at the time. If Led Zeppelin had announced that they were only going to play the blues, and they were going to play them quietly, I'd have still gone along and idolised them.

sixty-five

A FEW YEARS AGO I wrote a book about Scottish fairies. I am fond of fairies. I had not yet written about them at the time of the Led Zeppelin gig, but if I had, it would have gone like this:

Fluttering over the balcony the fairies looked down in amazement.

"I can't believe it," said Jean.

"Nor can I," said Agnes. "I've never heard anything like it."

"It is true what the newspaper said. Led Zeppelin are the best band in the world. And here they are in Glasgow playing at Green's Playhouse."

"How fortunate we chose this week to visit the city. Isn't that young man a very good guitarist? I've never heard such a skilful human musician."

"Me neither. Pass me the whisky, will you? Then let's fly onto the stage."

Afterwards, Scottish Fairy society was never quite the same.

Some years later, Jean and Agnes each had a daughter, Heather and Morag. They were the first Scottish Fairies to travel to New York.

sixty-six

"GOOD EVENING," SAYS ROBERT PLANT, as the cheering dies down at the end of the blues. As he greets us, the noise wells up again. The singer grins.

"I didn't think anybody was here…"

…more cheers…

"…anyway, despite the fact that we're a bit late in joining you in sunny Glasgow, we've been very busy, we've made a new album…"

There's a fresh outbreak of cheering. On stage, the band are friendly to each other, friendly and intimate, exchanging looks and smiles like lovers. I'm pleased to see how friendly they are.

"…anyway, to save further ado, this is a track from the new album. It's called… it's called… 'Dancing Days'…"

We applaud. The riff starts up, a grinding noise from the guitar.

For me, this is the first time that dancing days have ever arrived. I've never danced anywhere before. I wouldn't have danced at a nightclub, not that there were any nightclubs in Glasgow for fifteen-year-olds. There were school discos. I never danced at them. But now I dance. Cherry dances. Zed dances. The whole audience dances. The fairies dance. Led Zeppelin dance. Jimi Hendrix, watching from above, dances.

"It's true," he says. "Dancing days really are here again."

sixty-seven

ROADIES HURRY ON carrying four wooden chairs which they place at the front of the stage. Led Zeppelin like to do some acoustic numbers, sitting as close to the audience as possible. Jimmy Page straps on an acoustic guitar and John Bonham has a sort of tambourine with a skin over it which he plays with a single stick. John Paul Jones keeps hold of his electric bass and there's a short pause while they get themselves seated.

As Robert Plant is waiting for the others to get ready, he actually says, "Och Aye" into the microphone. This is the sort of thing English people often say as a sort of gentle mockery of the Scots, as if we all spoke like nineteenth century highlanders. But it's fine. Gentle mockery is all right when it comes from your heroes.

As he tries to introduce the song, the crowd's enthusiasm wells up again, and he has to calm us down.

"Shut up... hang on... listen..." he says, quite pleasantly. "Listen... this is a very important aesthetic part of the night's proceedings... because... hang on... shut up...' He gently chides the people who are making too much noise. The next sentence is lost as, rather counter-productively, we cheer Robert Plant for trying to quieten people down.

"So... eh... this is a song that was conceived in the...almost pure unaffected conditions of the Welsh mountains..."

...big cheer...

" 'Bron-Y-Aur Stomp'..."

...massive cheer. While it's wonderful to hear this with Led Zeppelin sitting only a few yards away like they're just rehearsing in the front room, in truth we're making so much noise that we don't hear that much of it. Jimmy Page does some guitar extravagances which are hard to catch, but we all howl in delight anyway.

By now people have expended so much energy in jumping that the seats start to collapse. Whole rows just crumple to the ground. The fans don't pay much attention, they simply clamber on the wreckage for a better view as security men battle their way through to try and fix things. There is the strange sight of bouncers trying to hoist entire rows of dilapidated cinema seats back into position while the audience keeps jumping up and down among the debris. Oblivious to the security men, oblivious to any danger of having their legs crushed, they just leap up and down to the 'Bron-Y-Aur Stomp'.

At the ends of the rows people teeter precariously on the backs of their seats and stretch up their arms to grasp hold of the boxes above, to balance themselves. Meanwhile, people in the balcony are clambering into the boxes and, from there, dropping to the ground. Glasgow was always an enthusiastic audience, but not like this. It's chaos. It's great.

Soon the bouncers give up trying to lift the seats and retreat from view. More rows collapse and people perch dangerously on the jagged metal frames, still dancing. Fiona puts her arms round Zed's neck and hoists herself up on his back to wave her arms in the air. Robert Plant catches sight of this and grins right at her. John

Bonham, a stocky figure in his small wooden chair, beams with satisfaction at the audience. He makes some private comment which makes the singer grin before he lumbers off to reposition himself behind his drum kit.

It's a mighty drum kit, though not the mightiest I've seen. Other groups have arrived at Green's with more drums. That didn't make any of their drummers sound as good as John Bonham, of course. That would just be a foolish notion.

Someone screams in my ear so loudly that I wince. It's Cherry.

"I love them," she screams.

sixty-eight

I ALWAYS REMEMBER CHERRY SHOUTING OUT, "I love them." She sounded wild and happy. She had never sounded like that before. I'd guess her life changed at that moment.

Manx wonders if being in love with a band is the same as being in love with a person. It sounds ridiculous at first, but on reflection, we are not so sure.

"It seems just as intense. I'm sure I loved Led Zeppelin when I was fifteen as much as I ever loved anyone since."

"But," ponders Manx, "do you get the terrible misery afterwards?'

Manx equates love with terrible misery. So do I. It is a strong bond between us.

Manx fell in love with the great love of her life who is never coming back because he bought 200 packets of breakfast cereal just to find the free gift she needed to complete her collection of plastic horses.

Each of these plastic horses was around two inches long. They were cheerful-looking animals. Manx collected the horses even though she could rarely manage to eat a whole bowl of cereal. She was around twenty-four at the time. There were ten horses in all, as pictured on the back of the cereal packet. Manx, after a lot of shopping, managed to find all ten. This might have been enough to make anyone completely satisfied, having all ten cheerful little ponies, but there was a problem. Seven of the horses were brown, two of them were black, and one of them was yellow.

"How does the yellow horse feel being the only one which is such a funny colour?" thought Manx, and felt quite unhappy about it.

"They should have made another yellow horse," she told her friends. "It's not right."

"Relax," said her friends. "You've collected the whole set. What more do you want?"

But Manx wasn't happy. She couldn't help feeling that in the herd of plastic horses she now had on the table beside her bed, there was some degree of loneliness.

"It must be terrible being the only yellow one. What if all the other horses laugh at it when I'm not around?"

So Manx kept on buying cereal. She amassed a huge herd of brown and black horses, but she couldn't find another yellow animal anywhere. She became very unhappy, and time was running out. The special offer would end soon. The cereal company would move on to a new promotion and there would be no more horses. Her therapy sessions switched rapidly from descriptions of her lonely childhood to the story of her ceaseless quest for another yellow pony.

I knew Manx at this time. I knew she was unhappy about the yellow horse but I never did anything about it. No one did anything about it apart from Andrew, who went to the supermarket with a van and bought every packet of cereal in the place, including the ones they had in the storeroom, took them home, emptied the contents out on a sheet in his front room, and eventually found another yellow horse. He took it to Manx. Her face lit up. She radiated happiness.

Afterwards, she was always in love with Andrew. She marvelled that he had understood how important this was to her. Not only had he understood, he had done something about it.

Andrew eventually left Manx for another woman. He never loved Manx as much as she loved him. It was a shame really that he had found the yellow horse. If he hadn't, she would never have fallen so hopelessly in love with him, and she would have got over the horse crisis eventually. She'll never get over Andrew.

"I'll never get over that one," says Manx, gloomily, and often.

"Yes Manx, we tried and we failed. The story of our lives. We better get back to Led Zeppelin quickly before things get too miserable around here."

sixty-nine

THE CHAIRS ARE REMOVED and the band get themselves organised again.

"This is a song that really encompasses everywhere that we've ever been... It's another track off, eh... off the new album... it's called 'The Song Remains the Same'..."

I'm touched here by a slight twinge of anxiety. Is it possible they might not play 'Whole Lotta Love' and

'Stairway to Heaven'? Then my life will be ruined. If Led Zeppelin don't play 'Whole Lotta Love' and 'Stairway to Heaven' it's going to be a disaster. Atlantis, so recently risen from the depths, will once more sink without trace.

'The Song Remains the Same' sounds like nothing I've ever heard before. As it builds up, Robert Plant maintains a silent, regal dignity beside the mike stand. When he isn't singing, he looks entirely happy on stage. He doesn't shuffle around in an embarrassed manner like some vocalists. He stands there relaxed, dancing a little, completely at ease. John Paul Jones, still with his bass guitar slung around his neck, moves back behind his banks of keyboards and starts playing an accompaniment on the Mellotron. He does this all night, shuttling between bass and keyboards. For some reason, while he's playing keyboards, it never feels like the bass is missing.

The number draws to a lingering close. I'm affected by it in a way uncommon for a song I haven't heard before.

"Was that all right?" says Robert Plant. Everyone screams that it was, and we howl so that his next words are drowned out.

Fiona has climbed down from Zed's shoulders and now stands beside him. Zed is in a world of his own. I can see that he doesn't want to be distracted but Fiona is insistent. She wraps some of Zed's curls in her fingers and draws his head round forcibly to kiss him. Once she gets his attention, they do seem to kiss for a long time. I glance round at Cherry and she's looking at Zed and Fiona and smiling. I wouldn't have thought she'd approve, with her passion for Zed. Perhaps she's just caught up in the frenzy produced by the overwhelming sexual energy that pumps out of Led Zeppelin.

I don't know if I approve. I don't like anything that causes trouble for Zed. But I do like anything that makes Suzy available. Unfortunately, Suzy is hanging back with Greg. I shake my head. I'll think about it later. With the first eerie notes of 'Dazed and Confused' rolling off the stage, there's no time to think about anything else.

seventy

"LOOK," SAYS AGNES TO JEAN. "Isn't that Jimi Hendrix up there in a Zeppelin?"

They wave to Jimi Hendrix. He waves back and smiles.

The fairies look down on the figures below and see Zed kissing Fiona and Greg holding hands with Suzy.

Jean, who has the second sight and can sometimes glimpse the future, shakes her head and turns to Agnes.

"I can see that something bad is going to happen tonight. Something very bad. Pass me the whisky."

seventy-one

I WANTED TO SAY TO ZED, 'stop kissing Fiona, nothing good will come of it,' but I couldn't say that, not to Zed.

I wanted to say to Greg, 'stop holding hands with Suzy', but he would have known I was only saying it from jealousy.

Sweat poured off me, drenching my T-shirt. None too clean to begin with, my T-shirt was now a damp mass of running ink and food stains. In those days, I often had food stains on the front of my T-shirt.

This hasn't really improved with age. In the harsh modern world, Manx has noticed, and told me off.

"Is it because you're a messy eater? Or do you just not wash your clothes often enough?"

"I don't know. Maybe it's a combination of the two."

Manx rubs her belly. We've seen a programme on TV about Egypt which has reminded her of the great love of her life who is never coming back, so now she's starting to hurt.

I don't want Manx to become bulimic again. She was a terrible bulimic when we first met. She would fast for days at a time, then go on an enormous binge, then make herself sick so she wouldn't have ingested too many calories. Calories were her deadly enemy.

She couldn't see her body in a realistic manner, the way everyone else saw it. What she saw in the mirror was a huge ugly, obese person that no one could love or even like.

It might have struck an observer as strange that this woman was confident enough to visit countries around the world in an adventurous manner, and yet could not manage to eat like a normal person. I wasn't at all surprised. I had long ago realised that society was placing such pressures on young women that they could hardly help being insane in their relationships to food. Anyone who is insane in their relationship to food has my immediate sympathy.

Manx has many large scars on her arms where she sliced herself open with a kitchen knife after she was overwhelmed with feelings of guilt and self-loathing. Since we became friends, her desire to mutilate herself has diminished, and on several occasions when the urge has been almost overpowering, I've managed to talk her out of it. Feel free to tell me about your food problems, if we ever meet.

146

The TV programme about Egypt didn't mention Nefertiti, which was a disappointment.

We've organised all the books and manuscripts into the categories as devised by Manx: the cover, the blurb, the first page, the author's financial statement, the author's photograph, and the statement of intent.

Awarding points in each category leads to a tie between a book written by a starving author which has a really nice blue cover plus a good joke on the first page, and a volume of poetry which also has a good cover with a picture of a tree. The poetry wouldn't have scored so highly but it was awarded the full extra ten points because the author is really pretty.

"She is extremely attractive," agrees Manx, studying her photograph. "She totally deserves the extra ten points in the 'anyone you might want to sleep with' category. So which one are you giving the prize to?"

It's a difficult decision, especially for a man with no formal training in literary criticism.

seventy-two

'DAZED AND CONFUSED' was one of the big numbers on the first album. This doom laden song was the soundtrack to which Greg and I would scan the skies, waiting for the attack of the Monstrous Hordes of Xotha. Their evil magic would cause the daylight to fade and darkness to descend as their dragon armies covered the sun.

"It's a lethal assault," screamed Greg, leaping for his war dragon.

"We have to defeat them," I shouted back, taking my lance in one hand and my sword in the other, and leaping for my own dragon. My dragon was younger than Greg's and not quite as powerful, but definitely more feisty. He was called Redfire and he came from a long line of princes of dragons. He was small and manoeuvrable, as dragons went, so I could fly underneath enemy dragons and roast their riders from behind, sending them off to their orcish hell.

Once, when I was out flying on my own, Redfire was brought down by a powerful new spell that Kuthimas had recently brought up from the depths of Mordor. I crashed behind enemy lines and it was excessively difficult getting home again. Evil creatures of every description constantly attacked us. My dragon had hurt his wings so we had to walk every step of the way. It was tough. So heroic was this episode that later it was made into a great epic ballad, and sung on special occasions. Yes, Redfire was a fine dragon. Greg's dragon was called Flaming Death, and he was a good dragon too.

Always, when we were under severe attack, 'Dazed and Confused' would be thundering out of the heavens, a perpetual soundtrack of mayhem and destruction as the uncountable enemy hordes threatened to swamp us and sweep the last vestiges of free civilisation off the planet. Without us, Glasgow would have been overrun long ago.

'Dazed and Confused' was always a popular phrase with Greg and me. We thought it suited our lives very well. No doubt every other Led Zeppelin fan in the world thought exactly the same.

As time passed, the live performances of 'Dazed and Confused' had grown and mutated so that by 1972 Led Zeppelin had fashioned it into a monstrous sonic assault in which the original tune was thrashed, distorted, attacked, assaulted, meandered through, improvised on, and generally pulled and twisted out of all recognition; taken to regions which were either tuneful or discordant, often hallucinogenic and, most satisfyingly, extremely noisy. Played live, 'Dazed and Confused' was a fuck of a lot of noise. When the first grim notes juddered out from the bass, the audience knew they were in for an onslaught of anything up to thirty minutes of tortured noise at immense volume.

This was fine with me. At the age of fifteen I was a great fan of tortured noise at immense volume. My ears can't take it so well these days.

seventy-three

ABOUT FIFTEEN MINUTES INTO 'DAZED AND CONFUSED', I have entered a different reality and am in a strange part of the universe where you can sit on the tail of a flaming guitar and fly through the sun. It's fantastic. Jimmy Page plays some weird improvised noise and as he does so he actually walks off the stage and says to me, "Hello I'm playing this bit just for you." Then he walks back over the heads of the crowd and keeps on playing, all without missing a note. It's awesome.

Jimmy Page takes out his violin bow and uses it on his guitar. This is another famous part of the Page repertoire, and the excitement caused by the sight of the violin bow makes Cherry grip my hand and squeeze my fingers.

After one or two slices of cacophonous noise, he takes the bow to the highest part of the neck and plays something which sounds very classical and intricate, and the crowd roar at his fine command of the fretboard. Then he's off back into harsh slabs of echoing noise and I'm heading back into the alternative reality where I can fly through the sun. In the alternative Led Zeppelin universe, Suzy is desperately in love with me, and it's her that is holding my hand. I like it here. I wish I didn't have to leave.

The band lurch into a funky rhythm, surprising us all. Apparently spontaneously, Robert Plant, John Paul Jones and Jimmy Page line up, step forward in time with each other and kick out one leg. They walk back, then forward, and do it again, a little dance step. So extraordinary is it to see the kings of progressive rock doing a dance step together that the audience gasps before bursting into another huge wave of cheering. The band grin at us, the rhythm mutates and reverts back to the metallic overload of 'Dazed and Confused', and they get back to being serious.

Years later, I relate this to Manx.

"I always remember Led Zeppelin doing that funky little dance step. It was so unexpected."

"Just another of these things that made them so terrific?" says Manx.

"Exactly."

"And made you love them even more?"

"Absolutely."

Manx is pretty familiar with my Led Zeppelin stories by now.

seventy-four

THE APPLAUSE for the twenty-five minute 'Dazed and Confused' extravaganza takes a long time to die away. Fiona has again climbed on Zed's shoulders and holds her hands out towards the stage. Cherry is still gripping my hand but I work my fingers free so I can wave my hands in the air. Streams of sweat run down my arms.

As the audience finally settles, Robert Plant adopts a slightly ironic tone and tells us that, "There's a guy who works for the *Melody Maker* who says Led Zeppelin's popularity has obviously waned..."

The crowd scream, to let the world know that this is not true. The band all smile.

Thinking about this now, it seems a little strange. Led Zeppelin had just sold out a huge tour of Britain. They regularly played to vast audiences all over the world. They knew how popular they were. Why did Robert Plant find it necessary to refute the journalist from the stage?

Perhaps, if ninety-nine per cent of the people you come in contact with think you are fabulous, it doesn't make up for the one per cent who don't like you. Maybe it just makes you worry about that one per cent all the more.

"Here's a song we wrote in a period that everybody decided we were doing nothing... 'Stairway to Heaven'."

The crowd erupts. 'Erupts' doesn't do our reaction justice. We explode into various parallel universes. We have been waiting for this, waiting for this all our lives. We feel satisfied.

seventy-five

'STAIRWAY TO HEAVEN', became Led Zeppelin's most famous song, a piece of music that soon came to represent everything about the band.

That was not surprising. For the Led Zeppelin fan it had everything. A nice slow build-up featuring flutes, keyboards and some intricate guitar. Lyrics well advanced in hippy mysticism. Drums that crashed in halfway through the song and beefed the whole thing up towards the end. A finale of fine wailing guitar and vocals. Uniquely for a Led Zeppelin song, the lyrics were printed inside the cover, so there was no problem in singing along. All in all, it was perfect.

Scorning the musical restrictions of the air guitarist, Greg and I would put on the record and play multiple imaginary instruments for the entire song. Even if we weren't actually listening to it at the time; for instance when we were sitting in class, we could still do a good version. I can remember feeling derision for another friend who, on attempting to join in with our imaginary rendition, actually brought in the drums at the wrong moment. An amateurish mistake, although to be fair, the point when the drums came in was quite tricky.

This was fine at the time but later it was a major problem. When punk rock swept away the old rock gods, 'Stairway to Heaven' was one of the most spectacular casualties. No song was more reviled. It symbolised everything that was bad about the old groups; their laser shows, their country mansions, their remoteness from their fans. 'Stairway to Heaven' became a joke, reviled on all sides by everyone, including me. I have never found any problems in reinventing my tastes to suit the moment.

It feels odd now, how important this all was. I listen to the fourth Led Zeppelin album a lot these days, 'Stairway to Heaven' included. It's not my favourite song but I still like it. I like the music and I like the lyrics. However, that is enough about 'Stairway to Heaven'. Any more and your attention will start to wander. I know, I've seen it happen.

I never play imaginary instruments any more, not even a single chord on an air guitar.

seventy-six

A GREAT FEELING OF RELIEF AND EXULTATION washes over me as I realise that I will now see Led Zeppelin play 'Stairway to Heaven'. I stop jumping up and down and let the introduction envelop me.

A few people in the audience are too far gone in their excitement to refrain from whistling and calling out, but most of us stand in reverence, entranced, as Robert Plant sings the gentle opening of the song.

The lights change to green, as if in respect to the pastoral nature of the lyrics. After Plant sings, he makes an ad-lib. He says, "Remember the forest?" and I know what he means. He means that life is all too complicated and too mechanical and we would be better off spending more time in forests. Well, that's what I think he means. I agree with him although I have never been in a forest. In Led Zeppelin Land I don't have to worry about anything, not even my painful love for Suzy.

The song lasts for a long time but it is still over too quickly. Near the end, Jimmy Page extends his guitar solo which brings me back into obsessive note-taking mode.

'He's extending the guitar solo,' I think. 'It's great.'

I'm sorry when it finishes. Everyone is. The audience has already made as much noise as it is possible for 3,000 people to make, and now we make more. The roar of approval stretches out without stopping. There is no limit to our pleasure at hearing Led Zeppelin play 'Stairway to Heaven' and we just keep cheering, clapping and stamping without any sign of ever coming to a halt.

Three chapters on 'Stairway to Heaven'. Great.

seventy-seven

THE LED ZEPPELIN GIG IN GLASGOW is such an incredible event that it affects all realities. Their music spreads out beyond, above and below the city, reaching the ears of all the Scottish creatures from this world and the next. Below the auditorium, deep in the sewers, the rats with their rat kings and rat queens look up in wonder, and crawl upwards to hear better. Ghosts of Vikings from the lands of ice and snow sail up the Clyde and march towards Renfield Street. They filter into the theatre without drawing their swords, just listening to the music, and as they hear Robert Plant scream out the word Valhalla they bellow in unison, and start to dance.

"The Vikings are dancing," say the fairies in the balcony. As they watch, another huge Zeppelin descends majestically into the auditorium, and Jimi Hendrix and Janis Joplin and Sonny Boy Williamson and Hank Williams float alongside it.

All the Scottish myths come to life and rush in. Dragons and griffins that last flew in the fourteenth century wake from their slumbers and burst free from their underground caverns to join in the revelry. The Sons of the North Wind, unicorns and naiads gallop from the woodlands on the Campsie hills, attracted to the city for the first time since Saint Kentigern preached there in the sixth century. Jacobite princes, Pictish warriors, Celtic bards, Highland clansmen, Border Reivers and Mull pirates are all drawn irresistibly towards Green's Playhouse, attracted by the cosmic powers of Led Zeppelin.

seventy-eight

"YOU KNOW, MANX, for some years now I have had to be careful about my stomach. It's really annoying. I used to be able to eat anything, or more to the point, not eat anything, and never have any problems. Since my stomach started misbehaving, I have to keep making sure I'm eating the right things, and not letting my stomach go empty. It's a total pain. I mean, who wants to be thinking about their stomach all the time? I don't want to think about it any of the time."

I muse gloomily on all the advice I've had from my own doctor, and the doctor at the hospital.

"It wasn't the advice I wanted to hear, not by a long way. 'Eat lots of small meals. Don't smoke too much. Don't drink on an empty stomach.' How tedious is that? It seems to me that if you get stomach pains then the doctor should just give you something to make them better.

"I mean, what are doctors for anyway? You just want them to make you healthy, not muck around with endless unwanted advice. I didn't go there to learn about diets, I just wanted my stomach fixed. How am I meant to look after my diet when I don't like food?"

And now I'm wondering about this whole procedure. Do these doctors really know anything?

"Consider the evidence. I spend days making sure I eat the right food, don't smoke too much, don't drink beer on an empty stomach and whatever else it is I'm supposed to do. And what happens? Stomach pains. But yesterday I met Frances, that young woman who emails me from Southampton University. She's a philosophy student and she never eats and she listens to music all the time and last year she put a long cut in her leg with a piece of broken glass. We had a pint at a pub in town, went to my house, watched videos, listened to music and finally retired to bed with a bottle of whisky, six beers and two packets of cigarettes. And what was the result of this behaviour? My stomach never felt better."

"So what you're really saying," says Manx, "is that if women, including for instance women twenty years younger than you, visit you in London and sleep with you on a regular basis, then you will receive great benefits in health?"

"Absolutely. Both physically and mentally. But try telling this to doctors and they won't go along with it at all. They just tell you to eat yoghurt."

Manx points out that even if the doctors did go along with it, it wouldn't really solve the problem.

"After all, it's not like they could prescribe you a regular supply of nurses."

I get a brief, happy vision of walking out of the hospital with a big prescription for nurses.

"I suppose not. Though I have often thought that as I'm always busy writing books that bring joy and happiness to the nation, the nation might do something in return. Providing me with lovers via the National Health Service would be an excellent idea. I'd be happy, confident and quite probably glowing with health. I'd write more books and everyone would benefit."

"What about the women?"

"They'd benefit too. I'd listen to their problems. And any young student that wants to travel all the way from Southampton to sleep with me is certainly riddled with problems. Young Frances hadn't eaten for forty-eight hours when she arrived in the pub. I got her to eat two packets of crisps and that's more than her nutritional therapist ever managed. I probably saved her life."

"So how's the stomach today?"

"It's gone bad again," I admit. "And Frances has gone back to Southampton, so I'm probably in for a prolonged bout of illness. It's a tough life, all in all, and getting older is really annoying."

seventy-nine

WE'VE BEEN DANCING and waving our arms about for an hour and a half. Heat pulses from our bodies. Green's Playhouse is now the only place of warmth in the whole frozen city. My T-shirt clings to my frame, soaked with perspiration. Cherry's face is wet and it shines as the lights wash over her. Her red hair, normally unruly, lies flat and damp over her neck and shoulders.

A hand grabs my shoulder and I struggle to turn my head in the crush. It's Greg. He's smiling. He puts his mouth close to my ear.

"The Monstrous Hordes of Xotha have been defeated," he says.

I smile back and nod vigorously. We are exultant. But this is the last moment that we are ever really friendly with each other.

Robert Plant's bare chest glistens under the spotlights. It's some time before he can make himself heard.

"This is a song we wrote when we first learned to sing in American…"

At the sound of the protracted opening chord, we scream. Jimmy Page pounds out the most famous riff in the world, as sung by us only that evening at the bus stop, the immortal opening to *Led Zeppelin Two*, 'Whole Lotta Love.'

The floor vibrates with the sound of the drums and the stamping of feet. As the riff for 'Whole Lotta Love' fills the auditorium, people lose control of themselves. Bodies pound against me in waves and I'm tossed this way and that until the weight of people behind forces me forward. The last remnants of the metal barriers are swept away and I end up pressed right against the stage, peeping over, my eyes level with the band's feet. Overwhelmed with excitement, fans start climbing onto the stage and the band's own security men rush on from the wings to throw them back into the crowd.

Crushed against the stage, I'm just tall enough to see over. When Robert Plant struts forward he is no more than six inches away. The people immediately behind me are stretching out their arms to touch him. I try to do the same but I can't free my limbs. I don't mind. I'm closer to Led Zeppelin than I ever thought I would be. Zed runs onto the stage and he manages to touch Jimmy Page before the roadies grab him and fling him back into the crowd, and as he sails overhead I can see him grinning.

I grin too because it's fitting that Zed will now be forever the boy who touched Jimmy Page. I open my mouth, put out my tongue, and I taste the stage. I don't know why I do this. It doesn't seem so mad at the time.

Fingers dig into my arm. I recognise the nail varnish on Cherry's small hand as she claws her way through to me. She has to haul herself up to see the band and she wedges herself against the stage, with her feet dangling in the air, held in place by the press of bodies.

As the riff breaks down into the psychedelic middle section, Robert Plant strides over to the theremin. He strokes the air around it and weird, banshee-like wailings fill the auditorium. The shrill electronic attack builds to a violent crescendo as Jimmy Page brings ever stranger noises from the guitar. He turns to face his amplifier so that great slabs of screeching feedback scream from the speakers. The bass and drums are still thundering along, unstoppable. At this moment, I am overwhelmed with the excitement so I turn towards Cherry and, as her face is conveniently pointing towards me only about an inch away, I kiss her on the lips and she kisses me back, quite forcibly, and presses her tongue into my mouth.

I feel good that the first time I've properly kissed anyone I'm only a few feet away from Led Zeppelin, and they're playing 'Whole Lotta Love'. I feel so good it doesn't strike me as odd that I've just kissed Cherry, because I certainly needed someone to kiss. As if they could read my thoughts, the band break into an old rhythm and blues song, 'Everybody Needs Somebody to Love'. The audience bounces up and down and Cherry loses her grasp on the stage and falls sideways into my arms, Robert Plant shrieks, long noises of sex and desire. The music suddenly stops and the singer berates a security man who is waving a torch and trying to drag fans away from the stage. Then the band gets back to their furious medley of old R&B and Elvis songs before crashing into 'Stuck on You', a blues of their own so heavy it seems like the weight of the notes might warp the stage beneath them. Cherry presses herself against me. Jimmy Page bends the notes and grimaces with the effort. We grimace in sympathy. I can feel the heat of Cherry's small body. She takes my hand and clasps it tighter and tighter through a long display of guitar playing so dexterous that the crowd can only stand amazed, worshipping the man. By the time the solo finishes, Cherry's nails are digging into my skin like a wild animal, and she turns her head and kisses me again, quite savagely.

"Jimmy Page, Jimmy Page!" says Robert Plant, and then 'Whole Lotta Love' starts up again like a train thundering into Central Station, out of control and heading for disaster. The perfect riff repeats on itself. Da-da da-da DA da-da da-da. The audience are maddened and swarm onto the stage. The security men fight to clear them away. There's a guitar break and a drum roll and then it's the end.

"Thank you very much! Good night!"

eighty

THE AUDIENCE BAYS FOR AN ENCORE. I howl with them, but I'm now slightly distracted because it's starting to sink in that I have kissed Cherry. She's still holding my hand and shows no inclination to let go. As my euphoria fades, I realise that things have not gone as I intended. The last thing I want to do is start a relationship with Cherry.

I withdraw my hand and look around. Zed is grinning at me. I grin back but it's forced. Zed told me to go out with Cherry. Obviously he's seen us kissing and holding hands and thinks it's an excellent idea. I'm not convinced. Cherry has risen in my estimation since her assault on the front of the stage. She certainly showed herself to be a much more active and determined Led Zeppelin fan than Suzy, who hung back, probably sulking. But Cherry isn't Suzy with the golden hair and no amount of enthusiasm for Led Zeppelin will make her so.

I imagine what would happen at school if people learned I was going out with geeky little Cherry. Everyone would laugh. My face grows hot as I realise that kids from school might well have seen us kiss. I take a step back to distance myself and, although Cherry is beaming at me, I avoid catching her eye, involving myself instead in shouting for an encore.

Bands always played an encore at Green's Playhouse, but sometimes it was a very perfunctory affair. If they hadn't been very good and the audience didn't care much one way or the other, the group would be back within thirty seconds. With Led Zeppelin it is just the opposite. The audience is screaming hysterically for them to return but the stage remains empty for a long time, far longer than was ever the case at any other gig.

Gig. An interesting word. It used to mean a sort of carriage, or a fool, or a whim, or a spinning top, or a flighty girl. *The Oxford Dictionary* doesn't know why it came to be used to mean a musical event. *Brewer's Dictionary* says it was first used by American jazz musicians in the thirties, but it doesn't know how the word originated.

The bouncers use this interval to reassert themselves at the front of the stage and we are forced backwards. Cherry sticks with me and we find ourselves next to Greg and Suzy.

"Fantastic!" he bellows in my ear.

I can sense that it's not just the band and the alcohol that's making Greg so cheerful. He's made progress with Suzy. Suzy is in a very bad mood about Zed and Fiona. She might well need some immediate comforting. Suzy's house is empty tonight, her parents are away. I hunt frantically for some method in which I might yet supplant Greg, and do the comforting myself.

So what I do is make some ridiculous comment about Atlantis rising from the waves to greet the Fabulous Dragon Army. Greg looks at me with pity, like a man who has now outgrown such childishness. Suzy ignores me altogether and turns her head towards the stage.

I curse myself for saying such a thing. In moments of high passion and excitement, I can never get it right.

Zed bumps into Suzy, and smiles at her, and starts ranting about Led Zeppelin. Suzy stares at him coldly and squeezes up to Greg. Cherry grabs me. She's put her glasses back on and looks excited.

"Can I join the Fabulous Dragon Army now?" she yells.

I hate her.

The audience is screaming. No one is giving up till we get an encore. When Led Zeppelin walk back onto the stage, Robert Plant is holding some flowers.

"Jenny's flowers," shouts Zed, cheerfully, and clambers precariously onto the remains of some ruined seats to dance. In Zed's world, nothing is wrong. He's still wearing his beloved afghan coat but has now taken off his T-shirt. He waves it in the air, a small but triumphant Led Zeppelin banner. His bare chest glistens like Robert Plant's.

Jimmy Page starts up the riff for 'Heartbreaker' and the crowd erupts again.

eighty-one

I IMAGINED AMERICAN SPACEMEN, orbiting the earth. They would have friends who had walked on the moon and relatives who were fighting in Vietnam. President Nixon was keen on both endeavours. The spacemen might have lost relatives in Vietnam, and these same relatives could have seen Led Zeppelin the year before they were drafted. If they'd lived in Philadelphia they'd have been part of an audience of 16,000 at the Spectrum. That was far more than could fit into Green's Playhouse, but none of the Glasgow audience were going to be killed in Vietnam. I read that 'Whole Lotta Love' was a popular song with the American troops in Vietnam, but I don't know if that's really true.

I imagined that as the astronauts passed over Glasgow, their instruments picked up strange and powerful readings. They looked down at Scotland, and wondered about the huge surge of power, but their instruments were not yet sophisticated enough to tell them what was causing it.

High above them, alien creatures, mapping the solar system, also paused and looked down. Their instruments were far more powerful so they knew all about the Led Zeppelin gig. Their instruments were so powerful they could read the posters on the walls and hear the music. They recorded it and sent it back to their native planet. Led Zeppelin were spreading throughout the universe.

eighty-two

I'M FURTHER AWAY FROM THE STAGE NOW. Suzy and Greg are still beside me. The sight of Suzy holding Greg's hand sends a poisonous arrow into my heart. Fifteen years old and already my life is finished. I am gloomy. Crushed under a flaming Zeppelin.

However, such is the amazing power of Led Zeppelin that, as soon as they start to play again, my problems start to fade. 'Heartbreaker' has this great bit where the music stops and Jimmy Page comes in with an extended piece of solo guitar. On the record it was always a high spot and live it's even better. It's a guitar solo like none other. It's a guitar solo to realign the planets and bring all parts of the universe into harmony. My anxieties melt away. The riff thumps back in. I've always liked riffs. If it's a good one, I like to hear it played again and again.

Riff. Another interesting word of uncertain origin. *The Oxford Dictionary* defines it as a short repeated musical phrase, derived from 'riffle', meaning a rippling motion. *Brewer's Dictionary* suggests it may just be an abbreviated version of 'refrain'.

When 'Heartbreaker' ends the band walks off and the lights go on but it makes no difference to the audience. We stay right where we are. This night will never be repeated and we are unwilling to let it finish.

Some of Jenny's flowers are still on the stage. Jenny will be pleased. I scream till my throat can't take any more. Zed gives me a drink from a small flask. It's whisky, far too powerful for my youthful palate. I cough and tears come to my eyes, but it revives my voice. A long time passes without any diminution of the crowd noise. The security guards look troubled.

It seems to me that there might be dragons above the stage, and maybe some other mythical creatures, waiting for the band to return. I don't mention this to anyone.

Eventually, the band stroll back on, smiling to each other and waving to us. John Bonham throws a drumstick into the crowd and there is a frantic scramble to get hold of it. Robert Plant has discarded his waistcoat and carries a cloth in his hand with which he mops the sweat from his face. They play 'Immigrant Song' and 'Communication Breakdown', both great favourites. I hurl myself forwards and get lost in the violent melée of bodies. Zed once more makes it on stage for a few seconds and, for the second time, achieves the honour of being thrown off by the road crew.

As this has been the greatest gig in the history of the world, it is fitting that the encore is also great. Both songs race by in a frenzy and when they stop, the crowd is exhausted; still triumphant, but ready to go home.

eighty-three

THE BAND HAS DEPARTED. Green's Playhouse has been badly ravaged. Many rows of seats have collapsed leaving only black metal spikes pointing upwards from the floor. The carpet is strewn with fragments of the chair coverings and a huge assortment of rubbish: bottles and cans, cigarette packets, ticket stubs, even items of discarded clothing.

Despite the elation of the event, the audience leaves quietly. We're drained of emotion. The gig has lasted longer than expected and most people have to hurry off for the last buses home. No one has a car. A few are picked up by friends or parents but the majority have to quickly switch from the ecstasy of music to the mundanity of public transport.

Outside the air is freezing and the warmth of our breath sends clouds of steam into the sky. My ears are ringing and I'm not thinking about anything much. The magnificence of the second encore has cleared my mind of everything. They played all my favourites. They played new songs that were terrific. They even sounded like they were pleased to be in Glasgow. The gig was better than anyone could have imagined.

Reality soon forces its way in. Outside the Playhouse Zed is arguing with Suzy. Most of the argument is coming from Suzy. Zed doesn't realise that anything is wrong. As far as he's concerned he has just been having a good time, watching Led Zeppelin with his friends. He looks perplexed as Suzy berates him about Fiona, though Fiona is nowhere to be seen. Greg is hanging back, and avoids catching my eye.

Zed listens to Suzy's tirade for a while before a look of anger crosses his face.

"What's the matter with you?" he demands. "You're never happy about anything. We've just seen Led Zeppelin."

"Well fuck Led Zeppelin," retorts Suzy.

Zed looks perplexed. He's embarrassed to be having this argument with Suzy in front of us, and embarrassed that she has insulted the band right after the gig. He can't cope with this right now. He's had too much fun, and he's drunk too much. He's still bare chested and his T-shirt is stuffed loosely into the waistband of his jeans. He doesn't want to stay around anyone who's going to insult his heroes, so he just turns away and hurries off. I last see him running down Renfield Street yelling out the words to 'Heartbreaker', his long dark hair billowing out behind him in the cold air.

"Come on," says Suzy, quite sharply, and she takes Greg's hand. They depart quickly in a manner which suggests that I am not welcome to follow.

Cherry plucks at my sleeve. I'd forgotten about her.

"Let's go home," she says.

We walk the short distance to the bus station in Buchanan Street. It's busy, with an assortment of other fans and late night drinkers, some people clutching posters from the gig and some eating chips wrapped in newspaper from the fish and chip shop across the road. There are ten minutes before the last bus is due.

"Wasn't it great?" says Cherry.

"Yes. It was great."

Now that there are just the two of us, I'm finding the recollection of our kiss more and more discomfiting. What if Cherry wants to do it again, right here? I scan the bus terminus for anyone I know from school. There are some people I recognise.

Cherry is looking eager. I think she does want to kiss me again. I don't know what to do. If it were not for the fact that we are waiting for the last bus, I might run away and hide, then catch a later one. I curse myself for kissing Cherry and pray that she will do the decent thing and never mention it again, just put it down to the over-excitement caused by Led Zeppelin.

I wonder where Suzy is. Has she really taken Greg back to her empty house? It's a very distressing thought. And where has Zed gone?

Cherry nuzzles up to me. She raises herself on her toes and tries to kiss me.

"Don't do that," I say, sharply.

Cherry looks crestfallen.

"Why not?"

I'm at a loss for an answer. I'm not equipped to deal with this sort of thing. In truth, the answer is that I think I'm too cool a guy to have any involvement with someone with such funny hair and glasses. I have just enough tact not to come right out and say this, so I remain silent. The night air is freezing, and as the heat from the gig leaves my body I start to shiver.

"Why not?" says Cherry again.

"Because I'm upset about Suzy going away with Greg," I blurt out.

"Suzy?"

"You know I'm in love with Suzy."

Cherry steps back. The eager look drains from her face.

"You certainly mentioned it enough times," she mumbles.

"Aren't you in love with Zed?" I ask, desperately seeking some way out.

Cherry shakes her head.

"Of course not."

We wait in silence for the bus. I feel bad. Some Led Zeppelin fans appear beside us, talking excitedly. Listening to their conversation reminds me of the good time I've had.

"I wonder if Suzy enjoyed the gig?" I say.

"Fuck Suzy," says Cherry.

I never heard Cherry say 'fuck' at any other time. She's starting to cry. She runs off, back into the night-time Glasgow streets. The bus arrives and I travel home on my own.

eighty-four

"SO YOU WOULDN'T SAY your first teenage kiss was a great success?" says Manx.

"Not really. Well, I suppose it was successful enough when it happened but afterwards I felt ridiculous. I mean Cherry? I'd spent the last three years being desperate for Suzy and now I'd somehow got involved with Cherry."

"Was she really so bad?"

"No," I reply. "But I had the strong conviction at the time that she wasn't good enough. Just too much of a loser for me to get involved with. As a long-term Led Zeppelin fan I was far too cool for her. After all, she only bought her first Zeppelin T-shirt the week before."

I pause. I can feel a general wave of old-girlfriend depression coming on.

"I do admit it was only me that thought I was too cool for Cherry. No one else in school would have thought that. I used to pretend I was flying on a dragon and visiting Atlantis. Hardly mature behaviour. Why did I think I was more highly rated than Cherry? And how did I ever imagine that I was going to attract Suzy?"

"Wasn't Cherry ever attracted to Zed?"

"No. She was attracted to me all along. It turned out the letter Z was just Cherry's code to keep it a secret in case anyone read her diary."

It's too hot. There's nothing good on TV. A full scale 'hopeless love affair' depression quickly settles in. I become despondent. Gloom descends like a thick black cloud, completely enveloping me. Damn. I should have been more careful.

"This is what happens when you take your mind off television and start thinking about the past."

I feel bad. I wish that it would rain for forty days and forty nights and the world would be destroyed in a gigantic flood.

Manx nods. Manx never expects love affairs to work out well. After all, she is no longer with the father of her baby. To make it worse, the father of her baby isn't even the person she dreams about, or misses the most. The great love of Manx's life disappeared to the USA a long time ago and he's never coming back.

eighty-five

ANDREW, THE GREAT LOVE OF MANX'S LIFE, doesn't feature in this book, apart from by way of explanation of her depression. She hasn't seen him in years. The last she heard he was married with two children, and teaching Egyptology at a university in Iowa.

Manx knows he is never coming back. He isn't one of these great loves that just might reappear in her life some time. Not one of those great loves that might, just might, ring the doorbell one day and say, 'well maybe we should get together again'. Rather, it's the sort of one true love that lies malevolently in your belly for the rest of your days, sometimes causing pain, sometimes almost forgotten, but always waiting there to rise up and chew on your heart if it ever seems like your life could be starting to go well.

I have one of those too. I wonder if everybody does. Jesmin, who teaches Manx's course in computing, is always complaining to Manx that she misses her old boyfriend. Poor Jesmin takes anti-depressants by the pound, as if the weight of them might crush the horrible dragon inside her that is always waiting to eat her up, but they never will.

"Do you think this all would have been better if I hadn't been such a joke at school?"

"Maybe," says Manx. "But you wouldn't have written any books."

This is true. Manx knows that I'm still trying to make up for my low status at school.

"Probably, if Suzy sees me being interviewed on TV she'll wish she'd gone out with me."

I'm always trying to make up.

Manx asks if I've come up with a winner in the literary competition and I reply that I haven't.

"Well, you might as well vote for the woman you want to sleep with."

"Yes, that seems most sensible."

"Have you read any of her poems?"

"No. I was going to last night but I watched *Buffy the Vampire Slayer* videos instead. It's a lot more fun than poetry."

eighty-six

THE LED ZEPPELIN GIG IN GLASGOW was the greatest, most famous, most talked about event in the history of rock music. But only by people in Glasgow. Elsewhere, it passed by largely unnoticed. It wasn't reviewed in the music papers. They were based in London, and chose to review other nights of the tour. The following year, Led Zeppelin would play to a crowd of 60,000 in Tampa. Glasgow couldn't compete with that. It was just another date and it didn't earn a place in the great Led Zeppelin mythology.

There are plenty of books on the history of Led Zeppelin; you can read about every gig they ever did. Some of these are legendary, like the time they played for four and a half hours in Boston, or the fabulous 1977 series of gigs at the Inglewood Forum in Los Angeles. None of these books has much to say about Glasgow. Some list it without comment, some don't even mention it.

In Texas, rich groupies hired their own private jet to follow the Led Zeppelin plane. In Denmark, Baroness Zeppelin threatened legal action against the band for using her family name. All over the world, startling things happened as Led Zeppelin moved around the globe, winning renown both for their music and their Dionysian excesses. No one tells stories of their time in Scotland. There are no legendary tales of hotel misbehaviour, no anecdotes that echo through the years. Nothing much seems to have gone on. Nothing to make it stand out.

However, this is simply because the rock biographers didn't turn up that night. The writers didn't happen to be there. So I have little evidence to corroborate my claims about the wonderfulness of the gig, although Luis Rey, in his huge history of Led Zeppelin live tapes and bootlegs, does say that the Glasgow gig is one of his favourites from that tour. He describes it as "an incredible performance for an amazing audience."

However, I can personally state that Led Zeppelin, on the 4th of December, 1972, at Green's Playhouse, was the greatest night in rock and roll history.

eighty-seven

WHEN I ARRIVED HOME my spirits had revived. The episode of Cherry was now closed. It had been a difficult situation but I thought I'd dealt with it well. Provided no one else actually saw us kissing, I'd probably get away with it. Cherry might be upset for a while but affairs of the heart were tough. You only had to listen to Led Zeppelin to know that.

Even the shattering disappointment of Suzy taking Greg home with her wasn't too bad when I though it through. There was very little chance that they would actually sleep together. Suzy still loved Zed. She might have been mad enough at him to walk away with Greg, but I just couldn't see her sleeping with him. It wasn't like my friends were always having sex. It was a rare event.

Suzy might even be disgusted at Greg's low behaviour in trying to take advantage of her when she was vulnerable. If she didn't realise how bad Greg's behaviour was, I would certainly point it out it to her. Things might yet turn in my favour.

This left me free to marvel at the greatness of the concert. I touched my posters and told them how much I had enjoyed it. My ears were ringing from the volume of the music and some of the riffs still seemed be playing inside my head. I liked that. Led Zeppelin had made everything just fine, as I knew they would.

I peered through my curtains. There was frost on the ground. Redfire, my dragon, was frolicking about overhead and I waved to him. So what if Greg dismissed the Fabulous Dragon Army as kid's stuff? To hell with him. I'd run the whole army on my own if necessary.

I went to sleep thinking about the gig and I dreamed about it that night; good dreams, with nothing scary.

eighty-eight

IN LATER YEARS, whenever the young thistle fairies Heather and Morag had been caught misbehaving, which they frequently were, their grandmothers would shake their heads in disapproval and say to them, "It's no wonder you are such a bad, disreputable pair of fairies. After all, what can you expect? Your mothers ran off to see Led Zeppelin play in Glasgow."

eighty-nine

NEXT DAY MY EUPHORIA WAS UNDIMINISHED. I flew to school in a Zeppelin. My ears were still buzzing and I felt wild-eyed and free. As I waited at the kerb for cars to pass, I waved to the drivers like Robert Plant walking on stage. I didn't meet anyone I knew on the way. No sign of Zed, Suzy, Greg or Cherry. Crowds of young children in purple blazers were making their way to primary school. They hadn't been to see Led Zeppelin. Poor kids.

"You should have gone," I said to two seven year olds. "It was fantastic... It was..."

I couldn't think of a better word. Fantastic didn't seem strong enough. I let my coat hang open to display my Led Zeppelin T-shirt. It was moulded to my body, creased, stained and slept-in. No T-shirt had ever looked so good. It would get me into trouble at school. That was fine. I would tell any teacher who objected that if they didn't like my Led Zeppelin T-shirt that was their problem.

I walked into school playing an imaginary guitar, just like Jimmy Page, and the first person I saw was Cherry.

"Wasn't that fantastic?"

Cherry walked by me without speaking, without even acknowledging me. My euphoria began to fade. It was a bad start to the day and I had a sudden premonition that things were going to get worse.

The corridors were crowded with kids who ran and screamed as they made their way to the classes where the registers were checked every morning. As I walked into my class, some people who had been at the gig saw my T-shirt and cheered. I grinned at them. Bassy made some flapping movements with his arms, part of his normal mockery about dragons, but I ignored him. Last night I'd been six inches away from Robert Plant, so who cared what Bassy did?

Suzy hadn't arrived yet, but Greg was sitting at the back of the room. He looked tired.

"Wasn't that fantastic?" I said, sitting next to him.

"Yes," replied Greg.

He smiled in a particularly satisfied way and yawned which, knowing Greg as well as I did, I interpreted to mean that he was claiming to have slept with Suzy.

I stared at him with suspicion.

"You're lying."

"No I'm not."

He wasn't. Greg and Suzy had really been in bed together. I reeled. After a very short initial flight, my Zeppelin seemed to have crashed in flames.

ninety

IN OUR FIRST CLASS OF THE DAY, Geography, Greg bragged about his night with Suzy. I hated him. I knew that I would always hate him. I took my eye off Suzy and my best friend for one minute and what happened? They went to bed together.

Suzy hadn't arrived at school. Probably tired out from sex with Greg. I tumbled into a bottomless pit of misery. I wondered if I should just go home. When Suzy finally arrived, late, she looked tired. Her blonde hair was disarrayed and her eyes were red. Some after-effect of fucking Greg, perhaps. She didn't look at him as she took her seat, and she didn't respond to the teacher's sarcasm over her late appearance. The teacher droned on. I stared at my chest, at my Led Zeppelin T-shirt. Life was useless. I could see already that it would never go right.

When the class ended Greg, rose quickly and worked his way through to Suzy. I hung back, not wishing to hear their intimate conversation. I put my head down and walked on without looking. Greg grabbed me as I passed. Suzy had already disappeared.

"She won't speak to me," he said.

"Why not?"

Greg didn't know. We couldn't understand it.

"Are you sure she wanted to do it?" I demanded.

"Of course she wanted to do it. She practically dragged me into bed."

"Probably just because she was so mad at Zed," I suggested, trying to deflate Greg. Greg wasn't stupid and this had already occurred to him. Even for inexperienced youths like ourselves, the notion of sleeping with one person to get revenge on another was easy to understand.

"I don't suppose she cared for me one way or the other. And now she won't speak to me at all."

Greg was depressed. His big love affair had certainly been more successful than mine, but it had ended after only a few hours. I was pleased that things had gone wrong. I still hated him.

At lunch-time, Greg asked me how I had got on with Cherry after we kissed. I had been dreading this. Greg knew I was secretly pleased about his discomfiture over Suzy and now he was about to get his own back.

I mumbled some inaudible reply.

"Bit weird isn't it, kissing Cherry?" continued Greg, laughing. "Did you take her home?"

"No," I replied, angry and humiliated. "She ran away and I got the last bus by myself."

For the first time it struck me that abandoning Cherry in the middle of Glasgow without any means of getting home, had not been very considerate behaviour. What had she done? Probably phoned her parents, which might get me into trouble if they blamed me for leaving her on her own.

We hung out at the school gate. More people arrived who had been at the gig, and talked about it with enthusiasm. I was relieved to get off the subject of Cherry, but unfortunately, she chose this moment to arrive on the scene. Normally Cherry would have skulked past the group, knowing that no one wanted her around, but instead of creeping by she strode up confidently and beamed at everyone.

"I met Led Zeppelin," she announced.

Everybody stared at her, amazed by the audacity of this claim.

"What do you mean you met Led Zeppelin?"

"Last night, I missed the last bus home and when I was wandering around I met the band in front of a hotel."

There was widespread derision at this. Out of all the people who'd been at the gig, there were a few who claimed they had made it onto the stage, and one boy who insisted he'd touched Robert Plant, and Zed of course had touched Jimmy Page, but no one was claiming to have actually met Led Zeppelin afterwards. It was absurd. We ridiculed her. Cherry seemed unconcerned. She didn't start snivelling as might have been expected. She didn't even blush. Instead she reached into her school bag and took out a flower.

"Robert Plant gave me this," she said.

Cherry walked off.

Everybody was mocking Cherry's ludicrous story until someone pointed out that Cherry, though undoubtedly a geek, an idiot, and a girl with really bad glasses, had never been known to lie. Immediately as these words were spoken, everyone knew them to be true. Cherry never lied. We fell silent, and the cold wind whistled around us.

"Cherry met Led Zeppelin?"

"Robert Plant gave her a flower?"

This had to be one of the most notable events in recorded history. Everyone wanted to hear the story of how Cherry met Led Zeppelin and there was a great stampede to catch up with her.

ninety-one

WHEN SHE RELATED HER STORY, Cherry mercifully left out the exact details of how she came to miss the last bus home. She did say that she'd had an argument with a boy but she didn't state that the boy was me.

People understood why she might want to be reticent

on the subject, and they also understood why such an argument might lead to her wandering the streets at night in tears. Everyone had learned by now that affairs of the heart were difficult.

Only the day before, the idea of Cherry being involved with a boy would have been reason for some cruel mockery, but not any more. After all, she was now a woman who'd spoken to Robert Plant. Her status was already rising. Why shouldn't she have a boyfriend?

Cherry had wandered around in the freezing rain, not knowing where she was going, till eventually she just stood on the pavement and cried about the injustice of life. A limousine drew up, further drenching her with water, and as the back door opened it knocked her down. Cherry found herself lying on the pavement in tears and the next thing she knew some young men with long hair were looking down at her with concern, asking her if she was all right. They assumed she was crying because they had hit her with the door, although Cherry admitted to us that really it hadn't been much of an accident.

She was helped into the foyer of the hotel by a huge bearded man – Peter Grant, the band's manager, we assumed – and John Paul Jones. Once inside, Robert Plant wiped the dirt off her face with a towel.

People gazed in awe at Cherry. Robert Plant had actually wiped her face. The adventure grew more fabulous all the time.

Led Zeppelin's reputation being what it was, everyone was naturally curious to learn if Cherry might have been invited to the hotel rooms for some Bacchanalian excesses, but Cherry shook her head. She didn't see any signs of Bacchanalian excesses, though they might have been going on upstairs. She was only in the foyer. It was all exciting enough anyway. All four members of the band had apologised to her for the accident, and when they saw her Led Zeppelin T-shirt and learned she'd been at the gig, they expressed pleasure at meeting such a dedicated young fan. Robert Plant had brought her some lemonade and given her a flower which he'd picked up in the dressing-room at Green's Playhouse. Then the hotel called a cab for Cherry and it took her home.

Jenny who worked in the flower shop later identified the flower, a gardenia, as very probably one of the ones which she'd placed in the dressing-room. Everyone believed Cherry anyway. She never lied and she hadn't exaggerated the story to unlikely levels.

So Cherry's stock rose immeasurably at school. She was always well-regarded for this incident. No one else had a story to compare with it. Robert Plant had brought her lemonade and given her a flower. You couldn't argue with that.

There was a part of the story that Cherry left out of the public explanation, a part which she didn't tell anyone at the time and only related to me some weeks afterwards. She said that when Robert Plant had asked her if she was hurt badly, as she was crying so much, being the honest soul that she was, Cherry replied that no, she wasn't hurt at all. She wasn't crying because of the accident. She was crying because she was in love with someone at school but this person had rejected her because she was a little geek, and not like the glamorous girls.

"Robert Plant said I shouldn't worry. He said I didn't look like a geek to him and anyway, quiet girls were always the most interesting. He told me he had a hard time at school too, but people that were shy and artistic like me always blossomed out and had fabulous lives afterwards. He said I had a lot to look forward to. And he liked my T-shirt. And he told me I shouldn't bother about what some stupid boy said because a better one was bound to come along soon."

I spent a long time wondering about this last part of the story. I could believe that Cherry had met the band. I could also believe that they had checked she was okay after knocking her onto the ground. But would Robert Plant really offer such comforting advice to young Cherry?

Well, maybe he did. Afterwards, Cherry certainly was a lot more confident. She had far less trouble relating to people at school. And if she was called a geek, which still happened occasionally, she didn't seem to mind. She was content to wait for her life to take off, as it would after school, just like Robert Plant said.

It was a good deal later that Cherry told me this. The day after the gig, she was so angry at me that she couldn't look in my direction without cursing under her breath.

ninety-two

SUZY WAS FEELING VERY BAD about sleeping with Greg. She had done it entirely to revenge herself on Zed. The next morning it didn't seem like such a good idea. She was overwhelmed with emotions of guilt, shame and self-loathing. Also, she was worried about her parents finding out.

It didn't take Suzy long to blame Greg for everything. It now seemed to her that Greg had taken advantage of her when her spirits were low, so she despised him. Greg was crushed. He'd lusted after Suzy for years and now, only a few hours after sleeping with him, she hated him. The only thing to do was to hate her back, which he did, but it didn't make him feel any better.

I had loathed Greg since learning of the affair. I was too jealous to hold it in and I criticised him bitterly. I pretended that I was upset because he'd stabbed Zed in the back by sleeping with his girlfriend but really, I was just maddened by envy. We fell out, quite seriously.

I tried being friendly with Suzy but that went wrong when Cherry told Suzy what a rat I was for kissing her and then treating her with contempt. Though Cherry was in a generally good humour after her encounter with Led Zeppelin, the good humour didn't extend to me. Suzy sided with Cherry and let me know that she didn't like me much better than she liked Greg. Cherry, already busy detesting me, naturally took Suzy's side against Greg and detested him as well.

The night before, we had all been out at the best gig ever, but by lunch-time everything was terrible.

In maths class we sometimes made little diagrams with arrows pointing this way and that. I sketched out a mental diagram of the current situation.

Suzy hates Greg
Greg hates Suzy
Cherry hates me
I hate Cherry
Greg hates me
I hate Greg
Cherry hates Greg
Greg hates Cherry
Suzy hates me
I love Suzy
Cherry and Suzy are still friends

I don't know where this would all have ended, but after lunch our teenage dislikes became irrelevant anyway. Suzy was called out of class for a telephone message.

182

This was a very rare event and we all waited with some trepidation for the outcome. No one ever phoned their child at school except in the most serious emergency. In our naivety, we wondered if Suzy's parents had found out that she'd had sex with Greg, and were coming to school to complain.

Suzy didn't appear back in class but she sent word to Cherry about what had happened, which Cherry transmitted to us at the afternoon interval.

"Zed's had an accident," she told us. "He was run down by a car last night and he's in hospital. Suzy says it's really serious and he might die."

So now there was really a lot of guilt, shame and self-loathing going on.

ninety-three

NEWS OF THE ACCIDENT spread through the school and a great misery descended on us all. Zed was unconscious, on a life-support machine. The doctors at the hospital couldn't say if he would recover or not. Suzy tried to visit as soon as she could, but only his family was allowed in to see him. She spent the next few days in anguish, waiting for news.

While his mother kept a vigil at his bedside, Suzy went over with Zed's father to the tenement in Byers Road where Zed had been living, to collect his belongings. Though it wasn't exactly stated, the implication was that Zed's father would not recognise his son's belongings and needed Suzy to help him identify them.

The distress and anxiety of Zed being on a life-support machine was unlike anything I had experienced.

183

Apparently, the accident had happened just after he'd left us outside Green's Playhouse, and I was tormented by the thought that only minutes after Zed had run off, still singing Led Zeppelin songs, he had fallen under the wheels of a car. I felt that I should have done something. I'd known Zed was upset. I knew he'd drunk too much. Maybe if I hadn't been so wrapped up in thinking about my own problems, I'd have gone after him and made sure he was all right.

If I was tormented by this, Suzy was driven near to madness. She blamed herself for the whole thing. If only she hadn't argued with Zed, he would never have run off. I did my best to console Suzy. Zed had been drinking and he was never careful when crossing roads. I didn't think it was reasonable for her to blame herself, but my attempted words of comfort had no effect.

Hostilities between Suzy, Cherry, Greg and me were suspended, if not entirely forgotten. In the light of Zed's accident, the falling out between me and Cherry seemed trivial and, though Cherry had still not forgiven me for crassly rejecting her, we started talking again. Similarly, Suzy needed friends around her and phoned me up to vent her anguish about Zed.

She still didn't feel much like talking to Greg. Although she didn't have the energy to remain so angry at him, sleeping together seemed to have put a permanent barrier between them. So with Zed close to death and Greg out of the picture, I ended up as Suzy's number one comforter after all. The irony of this was not very pleasing, or flattering.

"All it took," I said moodily, to my Led Zeppelin posters, "was for her boyfriend to be smashed into a coma and her preferred second choice to be forced out of the picture. Then Suzy turned to me right away."

A triumph. I had proved to be a strong third choice.

ninety-four

HERE IS HOW I CAME TO WRITE THIS BOOK. It was so many years after the gig in Glasgow that if anyone had asked me, I'd have said that Led Zeppelin had gone out of my mind. Too much music had happened since then for me to think about them any more. It wasn't till I went to have my navel pierced that I realised how important they still were to me.

I have four piercings for earrings. Ear piercing is quite painless. It's done with a little gun, and takes hardly any time. I was never nervous about having my ears pierced. However, I found that I was anxious about my navel. It might hurt. I had arranged to have it done in Brixton by an acquaintance who studied film and did body piercing as a sideline. He could see I was nervous, so he suggested that I should bring some music with me. Something that I would find comforting.

As I left my house, I picked up *Led Zeppelin Four* and put it in my bag. I hardly even thought about it. So it was that 25 years after the album was released, I turned up for my navel piercing with *Led Zeppelin Four* as my comfort music. We made small talk while 'Black Dog' was playing, and I got pierced to 'Rock and Roll'. If, for any reason, things had gone on longer, I might even have got pierced to 'Stairway to Heaven'.

So I realised that Led Zeppelin never stopped comforting me. It always lasted. Maybe not so intense, but still there, like those nagging teenage emotions.

ninety-five

I'M STARING OUT THE WINDOW at the small electrical goods shop across the street. Yesterday they put a sign up, announcing its closure. It's been forced out of business by bigger stores with cheaper prices. Soon it will be another empty store with windows covered with posters advertising gigs and a doorway full of crushed beer cans.

Manx calls me on the phone.

"Kemistry is dead. I just read it. She was killed in a road accident."

Manx is very upset by this. Although it had depressed her to look at pictures of the female DJ who was the same colour as her and had bleached hair like she used to and was having a great time playing music, it had also heartened her in a way. It made Manx feel that perhaps one day she would start enjoying her life again. Now that Kemistry has suddenly died, Manx takes it badly.

We read tributes on the internet which make us feel sadder. Poor Kemistry, killed so young in a car crash.

"Did Zed die after the accident?" asks Manx.

"I was fourteen when I saw Led Zeppelin," I reply.

"I thought you were fifteen."

"Well maybe fifteen. What's a year here or there? If I write the book, I might make myself twelve. I always like to take a little off my age. I think that's reasonable. It's not harming the public."

"Will you describe the whole gig?"

"No. I'd like to. I'd like to describe every single note and every word. But people would get bored. They'd put the book down and start watching *Buffy* instead. And who could blame them? It's such a fine programme."

It's the book judging soon. As Manx has sorted out my results for me, I've asked her if she'd like to come along.

"I'm too depressed," she says.

"Stop being depressed."

"Just like that?"

"You could give it a try."

We sit in silence.

"How about wearing the Nefertiti hat?"

Manx shakes her head.

"I wouldn't look as good as Kemistry anyway. She looked so good. I can't believe she's dead."

ninety-six

ZED REGAINED CONSCIOUSNESS, and the weeks passed. Greg, Suzy, Cherry and I were ecstatically happy when Zed came off the critical list, and we knew that he would live. We still weren't allowed to visit him. Only his family were, and we received little news, though they told Suzy that he was making a good recovery.

Eventually we were permitted to see him. Suzy went with Zed's parents, and Greg and I visited the next day. It had been six weeks since the gig. Christmas had come and gone and the ground was still frozen. We were feeling some trepidation. Suzy hadn't called to let us know how Zed was when she saw him, but his mother assured us that Zed would be pleased to see us. Zed's mother was full of love for her son. So was his father. Now that he'd been run down by a car, they couldn't love him enough.

I met Greg at the bus stop. We weren't such good friends any more but we forgot our differences for the day. We made the journey to the hospital to visit Zed, the coolest boy in school, our hero. We took fruit; grapes, oranges and bananas. We asked at reception where Zed was and a nurse lead us along a corridor. The corridor was very bright. It made me feel uncomfortable. I'd been in this hospital once before, to have my arm set after I broke it. It hurt.

Outside a green door we encountered Zed's mother. She was pleased to see us, and smiled. She shepherded us into the room.

As we entered, Zed's father was sitting by the bed trying to spoon some baby food into the mouth of someone I didn't recognise; a funny looking young person whose head seemed too heavy for his neck and who couldn't manage to get his mouth to connect with the spoon. Mashed potatoes and saliva trickled down his chin.

It was Zed. His hair was short, shaved for his operation. You could still see the lines of stitching on his scalp. He was propped up in bed wearing blue striped pyjamas and a blue dressing gown. I'd expected him to be wearing his afghan coat. There seemed to be something wrong with his right arm. He held it in front of him in a crooked manner and it shook, as if he couldn't control it properly. Sometimes it would jerk up and hit the spoon, sending more food cascading over the blankets.

I couldn't understand why his head kept jerking about. And his face was different. It was thinner, but it wasn't just that. His jaw hung slackly, like he couldn't remember how to hold it in place properly. Greg and I froze before we reached the bed. We stared with horror at the terrible sight of Zed, our beloved Zed, struggling to bring his mouth into contact with a spoonful of mashed potatoes while his lips twitched and his arm jerked and spittle collected on his chin.

His father muttered something that might have been encouragement, and kept trying to feed him. Zed's eyes were bright, wide open, and his mouth formed an idiot grin as he turned his head from side to side, apparently at random.

No one had told us that Zed was severely brain damaged. He was never coming home again, at least not in any form we'd recognise.

There was a plastic wind-up toy on the bed, the sort of thing a four-year-old might find amusing. Zed lost interest in the spoon and tried to push the toy with his shaky, crooked right arm.

"Your friends are here to see you," said his mother.

She looked at me encouragingly. I tried to smile back but all I could manage was a grimace that froze on my face like a death mask. Zed, the coolest boy in school, had turned into a spastic.

ninety-seven

I'M STANDING WITH GREG at the bus stop in Auchinairn Road, waiting for the bus home to Bishopbriggs and the bus won't come. We wait and wait. The cold rain turns into sleet and the wind blows it under the bus shelter and we stare out at the grey world with complete despair, just wishing that the bus would come and take us far away from the hospital.

We don't say anything. Since we left the hospital we haven't exchanged a single word. The language to cover what we might want to say doesn't seem to have been invented. I'm still young enough to not want to cry so I'm concentrating on not shedding any tears. As the sleet slams into my face, I lose some of my self-control and a few tears mix with the dirty Glasgow weather.

It seems like the bus will never arrive. I never waited so long. Cars speed by splashing us with freezing water from the puddles on the road. My greatcoat is wet and heavy and hangs round me in a shapeless bundle, and the water seeps through to my Led Zeppelin T-shirt. I wore it to cheer Zed up. I thought he'd like to see a picture of his heroes. He didn't recognise the picture. I don't think he could read any more. He didn't really recognise us, though his mother tried to pretend that he did. She made us promise to come again soon.

We wait, in the freezing cold, without a single word to say to each other. We're thinking about Zed propped up in his hospital bed, jerking his arm around, hanging his head and dribbling food over his chin, and playing with his plastic toy. I feel angry with his parents for dressing him in such a horrible pair of striped pyjamas. Zed would never have worn anything juvenile like that.

When the bus finally arrives, we troop on and sit with our faces pointed at the floor. It trundles home through the rain, stopping frequently, and everyone who boards the bus is cold and unhappy. The Christmas spirit has quickly evaporated. As I get off the bus I decide that I will one day write about my friend Zed, and inform the world that before he got his head smashed by a car, he was a really great person.

I call Suzy but she has gone to stay with her aunt in Newcastle, and her mother says she won't be back for a while.

ninety-eight

"I'VE FIXED YOUR ROBOT," said Cherry. She pushed a little button and the robot sprang into life. Zed looked at it with vague interest. His shaking arm reached out briefly before something else caught his attention and his gaze wandered across the room.

Cherry had repaired the robot and brought it to Zed, hoping that it might amuse him as he lay in his bed. Zed's mother appeared with a tray of tea and biscuits for us. When she saw that Cherry had brought the robot, and it was working, she broke down in tears and ran out of the room.

Cherry managed to be cheerful in the ward. The moment we left the hospital, she started crying. So did I. I was glad of the opportunity.

That night I dreamt that I was sitting under a tree beside Zed. The sun shone through the branches and there was a stream running gently by us. Zed was holding a tambourine. Instead of tiny metal cymbals it had green leaves and pink flowers. He shook it and music came out from the leaves and flowers.

Next day, I phoned Cherry to tell her about my dream and she invited me round to her house. I arrived just as Phil was leaving, violin case in hand. He greeted me stiffly. I don't know what Cherry had told him but Phil, the super-intelligent boy, probably guessed that the object of her affections had turned out not to be Zed, but me. This was a cruel piece of misfortune. He'd confessed his love for Cherry to the very person who stood in the way of it. Poor Phil.

I sat in Cherry's bedroom, drinking tea. She had a poster of the periodic table on the wall, displaying the atomic structure of all the elements. We talked a little

191

about Zed, but not much. It was too painful to talk about for long. We listened to records, without speaking.

"Do you think a huge Zeppelin might fly around to every Led Zeppelin gig?" I said, after a while.

"Yes," said Cherry.

"Really?"

"Yes."

We sat in silence, musing on this.

"Do you think there really is an Atlantis?"

Cherry nodded. She was sure Atlantis was out there somewhere.

"I think Led Zeppelin probably come from Atlantis," she added.

I was impressed. The possibility that Led Zeppelin themselves might actually come from Atlantis hadn't occurred to me. It would certainly make good sense. Cherry was far more sensible than I had ever imagined her to be. I liked her a lot more these days.

ninety-nine

AROUND THIS TIME, LED ZEPPELIN released *Houses of the Holy.* Cherry and I went into the centre of town to buy a copy each. It was good, going to buy a new Led Zeppelin album and having a girlfriend at the same time. Afterwards, I accompanied Cherry to the musical instruments shop in St Vincent Street where she picked up a new set of violin strings. Cherry didn't like playing the violin any more and was thinking of giving it up. This would mean arguing with her parents but Cherry thought she was about ready to argue with her parents.

I admired Cherry's skill on the violin. I didn't think she should stop playing but I didn't try to dissuade her as Cherry seemed quite determined. Playing the violin no longer fitted in with her self-image. She'd abandoned her glasses and grown her hair very long, and her Led Zeppelin T-shirt was now worn and faded with mystic symbols hand-painted on the front and back. She had a bag made of denim patches and wore a string of yellow plastic beads.

I was obliged to love *Houses of the Holy* because it was a new Led Zeppelin album, but secretly I was disappointed. It didn't seem to be momentous enough and I didn't like it that one of the song titles contained a reference to a joke. I was too serious to approve of musical jokes.

The track was called 'D'yer Mak'er'. The joke to which it refers goes as follows:

"My wife's just gone to the West Indies."
"Jamaica?"
"No, she went of her own accord."

Actually, I've always thought that was a good joke. However, it wasn't suitable for a Led Zeppelin title. You can't lead the Fabulous Dragon Army against the Monstrous Hordes of Xotha with some fool telling jokes all the time. It's bad for the concentration.

But possibly this shows that Led Zeppelin weren't as deadly serious about everything as their fans were. Unlike us, they could appreciate a joke.

I heard that Suzy made some jokes about Cherry and me, being such a geeky couple, and so did Greg.

I went out with Cherry till we both left school, and it was quite a happy relationship. We both got seriously drunk for the first time in each other's company, and we both experimented with drugs. We were still experimenting in 1975 when we bought *Physical Graffiti,* Led Zeppelin's monumental double album. We both loved this. It was a fantastic record. It still is. The cover showed a tenement in New York, which looked quite like the tenements in Glasgow.

Along with their massive success, Led Zeppelin attracted a great deal of criticism. Music journalists never really loved them, and would say that they failed to credit blues musicians for their songs, that they were a rock dinosaur, they were the product of management hype, there was no subtlety in their music, they were obsessed with power and volume, they were remote from their audience and anyway their audience was entirely made up of stoned juveniles.

I could say something about all of these criticisms if I wanted to. Some of them I would refute. Some of them I might say were true. But I'm not going to say anything about them. After all, I'm not a music journalist. I don't have any desire to persuade anyone that Led Zeppelin were any good. You can think whatever you like.

You either feel it or you don't. The same as any music. The same as any art. You feel it or you don't. The same as being in love. You can't be persuaded. You either feel it or you don't. I'm not going to try and change anyone's mind.

Led Zeppelin. Greatest rock band in the world, oh yes.

one hundred

"SO WHAT HAPPENED TO ZED?" asks Manx

"He died, after a while. It was a shock. He wasn't expected to live and then he wasn't expected to die, but he did. About a year after the accident, he just died in his sleep. I was pleased. I thought it was probably for the best. When I was younger, I thought it would be better to be dead than to be brain damaged. Now I don't know."

Manx nods. It's easier to be certain about things like that when you're young.

I'd kept on visiting Zed, with Cherry. So had Greg and Suzy, though everyone's visits became less frequent.

"I got bored visiting, after a while. It all seemed so useless."

Relating this to Manx, I still feel ashamed, but it's true. At first I was at the hospital every chance I could get, but after a few months I started going less often. It seemed hard to remember that the person in the hospital bed had once been my hero Zed. Zed's state of health never improved. He never really remembered who I was.

After a while my distress was replaced by a sort of emotional numbness and eventually my adolescent life just took over again, leaving little room for visiting the sick. Although I felt some secret relief when Zed finally died, I also felt shame that I hadn't visited as often as I should. My compassion had turned out not to be endless. I didn't feel good about it.

Poor Zed. I remember him much more fondly than Suzy. Suzy's hospital visiting record was about the same as mine. It started off frequent and then tailed off. During this time, she stopped being so friendly with me.

After Zed died we more or less ceased to be friends though we were still at school together. It was like she didn't want to be reminded of her ruined boyfriend.

I was buffered against this by my relationship with Cherry but it still hurt. I yearned for Suzy for a long time, far longer than I should have. I don't know what happened to Suzy after she went to university. Something fabulous, perhaps. Unless she was one of those people who were successful at school and then went on to have a tedious life, marrying another early achiever and settling down in the suburbs.

I was never really friendly with Greg again. I always hated him for sleeping with Suzy. I went to gigs with Cherry instead, and I noticed that Greg stopped going so frequently. At one time, Greg would never have missed a concert in Glasgow, but in the year that followed the Led Zeppelin gig he seemed almost to lose interest in music. By the time I left Bishopbriggs we had hardly spoken for months. Cherry replaced him as joint leader of the Fabulous Dragon Army and she was very good at that. We chased the Monstrous Hordes of Xotha from the sky.

one hundred and one

CHERRY WENT ON TO BE SUCCESSFUL. She attended university in Edinburgh. He parents had wanted her to stay in Glasgow but Cherry had never been quite the same since the Led Zeppelin gig. She was now far too confident to do anything she didn't want to do. She had long ago abandoned the violin and while at university she wrote, edited and produced a feminist newsletter. After she completed her degree in English, she took a job as a junior reporter on a local newspaper. She worked her way up and moved on to a staff writer's job in Manchester. From there she became assistant editor of a Sunday supplement in London and after that she was made editor of a large woman's magazine, *Elle* or maybe *New Woman*.

I noticed in a newspaper some time ago that she'd gone to New York and was editing a fashion magazine there, a very influential position. If you want people to come to your fashion show in the USA, you'd better be nice to Cherry, one of the new queens of American journalism.

She was a great girlfriend, fun to go out with. I have very good memories of Cherry.

one hundred and two

THE 133 BUS comes all the way from Tooting, passing through Streatham, Brixton and Kennington before crossing the river at London Bridge. After that, it turns east and goes onto Liverpool Street Station. I get off at London Bridge and walk to the institute where the judging is to take place. There I meet the two other judges and a man from the British Council who is there to take note of our opinions.

Later I meet Manx in town and she asks me how it went.

"It was tough," I admit. "The other two members of the panel surprised me. They'd read the books. I thought that was pretty unreasonable. I was expecting everyone to turn up without having bothered to read anything and just sort of award the prize to someone at random but no, they both had notes and opinions and wanted to discuss every damned thing. To make things worse, the person from the British Council kept asking questions. It was a trying experience. It took every ounce of my imagination to make it appear that I'd read the stuff. At one point, they got into some detailed discussion about the surprise ending of a historical novel and I was reduced to feigning a fit of coughing."

Manx agrees that this all sounds harsh.

"I had to slip the book into my pocket and visit the bathroom to examine the last page. Then I insisted we should have a tea break, which gave me an opportunity to sneak a look at some of the poetry. I said liked the poetry much better than the novels and that got me through in the end. You can just read a line and give an opinion and who knows if you only made it up that second?"

We go into a comic shop in Oxford Street and look at some comics, then Manx finds a large display of dolls from *Buffy the Vampire Slayer*. There are figures of Buffy, Willow, Xander, Angel, Spike, and some others. We're entranced.

"Did you give the prize to the woman you wanted to sleep with?" asks Manx.

I shake my head.

"No, it turns out she lives with her boyfriend so there wasn't any point. Though I still might have if it hadn't been that the other judges were really impressed with a poem she'd written about her mother going to see Led Zeppelin when she was young."

"Her mother went to see Led Zeppelin?"

"That's right. Twenty-five years ago. And has been droning on about it ever since, according to the young poet. The poem was quite angry about the whole thing. Suggested that anyone found guilty of boring the youth of today with stories about old rock bands should be sent into exile."

"What a bitch," says Manx.

"Absolutely. I was outraged."

Manx slips a Buffy doll off the shelf and into her bag. She asks if the poem was any good.

"How would I know? I used to think Cherry's poems were terrible and then when we started going out I thought they were good. Anyway, I voted to give the prize to another poet who wasn't so offensive."

"Was she pretty?" enquires Manx.

"Yes, quite pretty. I'll have to read some of her poems before the awards ceremony."

Manx slips a Xander doll off the shelf and into her bag. I sigh. Back when I was at school, I'd never have been so blasé about any form of art. I'd have read every word carefully, given my full attention to the task, and arrived at the judging with a well considered opinion. I would have cared.

"I'd like to buy all these Buffy dolls and play with them. I'll have time on my hands soon, I've almost finished the Led Zeppelin book. I'm at the 'nice and big' stage."

"What's the 'nice and big' stage?"

"I go through the text making sure I haven't used any long words. If I find any fancy adjectives have crept in, I replace them with small words like 'nice' and 'big'. I've liked these words ever since I was told not to use them in English class at school. After that, I check that the sentences are short so as people won't get confused and I shorten all the chapters so they won't get bored. I can't read anything complicated these days, my attention span is too short. Everyone else probably feels the same."

We take the 159 back home. There's a free listings magazine lying on the seat and I notice that next weekend they're showing *The Song Remains the Same*, the Led Zeppelin film, at a cinema in Brixton. I ask Manx if she'd like to come and see it with me.

"I won't have time, I'm still trying to finish the animation."

Our expedition into town has put Manx in a good mood, but the thought of struggling on with her work brings her down again.

one hundred and three

OFTEN PEOPLE ASK ME FOR ADVICE on how to get their books published. I would like to be helpful but it's difficult to give any useful advice. I don't have any contacts in the publishing world, and I have had my share of problems with publishers in the past.

So, apart from telling these people to try and find a good agent, which in itself is not an easy thing to do, I am unable to be very helpful.

But I have one piece of good advice. Sometimes you will find yourself in a book shop, looking round. You may be discouraged by the incredible range of titles on offer. Each of these will have favourable quotes on the back from journalists, often from impressive-sounding newspapers and magazines. Some of the books would seem to carry such a weight of acclaim, from the size and reputation of their publisher to the incontestable merit of their supporters in the press, as to make you think that you could never compete with them.

If this happens to you, do not worry. None of these people know any more than you. In fact, burdened down as they are with the necessity of making money for their companies, or rushing in articles to their editors, they know less. If you have just come out from seeing the band you always wanted to see and it has had such a beautiful and devastating effect on you that you just have to go and write it down, what you write down will be much better than anything an editor or journalist could do.

Led Zeppelin at Green's Playhouse in 1972. It was the only time they ever played in Glasgow. I am so pleased I went to that gig.

one hundred and four

MANX FINDS THAT HER SPIRITS ARE RAISED by the Buffy dolls.

"Every time I got depressed, I got the dolls out and played with them and it really made me feel better. And then Malachi played with them and he was quiet for hours so I got lots of work done. I've finished the tree-turning-into-dragon animation and made a start on the next project."

"Well done Manx, it's a triumph of the human spirit. Can you come to see the Led Zeppelin film now?"

Manx says that she can, so I call round and wait with the baby-sitter while Manx gets ready. It takes her a very long time to dress and do her make up and even then she isn't satisfied.

"I should wear something which looks like I'm celebrating."

"I suggest the Nefertiti hat. No other garment will fit the bill."

Manx brings out the hat and studies it dubiously.

"I don't think my spirit is strong enough wear this any more," she says.

"Nonsense Manx. Aren't you the woman who just stole Buffy dolls and finished your project all in one week? How many people could do that while looking after a baby? You have a very strong spirit."

Manx puts on the hat. It makes her look fabulous and it reminds me of the first time I ever saw her. During the short walk to the cinema everyone stares at her.

"I'm feeling uncomfortable," complains Manx. "I wish I hadn't worn this stupid hat."

Two young girls gaze at Manx as we pass. One of them calls out, asking where she got the hat, because she wants one as well. When Manx informs her that the hat was specially made for a theatre, the young girl stares wistfully at it, and wonders if she might find someone to make one for her. She says it would be the perfect accompaniment to her Dance Hall Queen outfit.

By the time we reach the cinema, Manx is feeling a little better. A young man approaches us with a camera in his hand.

"I'm doing an article on street fashion for *Vogue*," he says. "Would you like to be in it?"

I stand aside while the photographer takes pictures of Manx. On the small patch of grass outside the cinema, the assembled down-and-outs look on appreciatively. Manx is not shy in front of a camera. She likes being photographed and poses without inhibition.

We enter the small cinema and queue for tickets in the foyer. A woman, who turns out to be the manager, engages Manx in conversation and, before we can pay for our tickets, she says that we can come in free because Manx's hat is so great it has brightened up the place. We thank the manager then take our seats. They're comfy, old-fashioned seats, rather like the ones in Green's Playhouse all those years ago.

"Public reaction to the hat has been universally favourable," I whisper.

Manx smiles. Manx is now happy, the first time I've seen her happy for almost two years. I expect that tomorrow she will be unhappy again, but a few hours away from her problems will help her more than she realises.

The lights go down. The opening credits roll. A huge Zeppelin floats across the screen.

"Do you think Kemistry might be flying around in the Zeppelin?" says Manx, unexpectedly.

"What, being the new DJ?"

We think about this, and imagine the dance floor on the Zeppelin suddenly heaving under a violent sonic attack.

"She might have a new DJ partner."

"Queen Nefertiti, maybe?"

"Nefertiti would be good."

"Who's the new DJ?" asks Jimi Hendrix.

"It's Kemistry," replies Janis Joplin. "She just arrived. Quite a sound. Do you like it?"

"I sure do. The old Zeppelin is really rocking."

As the film starts, I wonder where Suzy is now, and I feel some echoes of my long-ago unhappiness over her. It fades as the band start to play. *The Song Remains the Same* still isn't that great a film, but it does feature Led Zeppelin on stage. You can't argue with that.

Acknowledgement

The newspaper report on page 63 is from *Led Zeppelin: The Concert File* by Dave Lewis and Simon Pallett. (Omnibus Press, 1997.)

CODEX

CODEX

www.codex-books.com

Shamanspace

by Steve Aylett

£6.99UK • $12.99USA • $19.99CAN/AUS • ISBN: 1 899598 20 0

God has been found to exist and the race is on to take revenge...

Opposing groups of occult assassins compete to exterminate the creator, with young gun Alix the favourite. As multidimensional war is waged, Alix travels through sidespace to confront the source of evil at the risk of destroying the universe.

   Shamanspace is an alchemical conspiracy adventure from Steve Aylett, author of *Slaughtermatic* and *Atom*.

'*A fluorescent cocktail of cynical adventure.* Shamanspace *explains why we're here, what it's all for, and why we should try our best to kill it as soon as possible*'
– Grant Morrison creator of *The Invisibles*

'*As exciting as an adrenaline rush*' – SFX

<www.shamanspace.com>

CODEX

www.codex-books.com

My Fault

by Billy Childish

Paperback

£8.95ᵤₖ • $16.95ᵤₛₐ • £24.95ₐᵤₛ/ᴄᴀɴ • ISBN: 1 899598 18 9

Hardback

Limited edition: 100 signed & numbered • £20.00ᵤₖ • ISBN: 1 899598 21 9

Also available: 26 hardbacks, original painted covers by the author, signed and marked A-Z • £50.00ᵤₖ

Hardback editions are available by mail order only.

The new, extensively revised edition of *My Fault* is both harrowing and hilarious. Referred to by Childish as a "creative confession", it is autobiographical fiction of the most poignant and intimate kind. In this powerful debut novel, Steven Hamper, Childish's alter ego, struggles through an abused childhood, to emerge rebellious and misunderstood, in a world distorted by alcohol, bullies and yes-men.

Childish began *My Fault* in 1982, writing about his relationship with his then girlfriend Tracey Emin (fictionalised as Dolli Bambi in the book). He continued writing over a fifteen year period, dredging through memories of his childhood and moulding them into the earlier parts of the novel.

Childish was a founder of the recent Stuckist art movement, and has exhibited his paintings worldwide. He has recorded more than 80 independent albums, with Thee Headcoats and other bands, and regularly tours Europe, Japan and the USA.

'Written with wit and passion, it has a rich vein of cruel humour running through it' – The Independent on Sunday

CODEX

www.codex-books.com

"i'd rather you lied" Selected Poems 1980-1998

by Billy Childish

£9.95UK • $17.95USA • $24.95AUS/CAN • ISBN: 1 899598 10 3

Illustrated by the author

Selected from over thirty published collections, *"i'd rather you lied"* brings together a lifetime's work of one of the most remarkable and unorthodox voices of the late twentieth century.

Accompanied by woodcuts and drawings from now rare or unobtainable originals, this volume sees Billy Childish take his rightful place as the poet laureate of the underdog.

'Raw, unmediated, bruisingly shocking' – The Daily Telegraph

'A self-made intellectual of a particularly English stripe, Mr Childish has sworn loyalty to populist art at its rawest' – The New York Times

www.codex-books.com

Notebooks of a Naked Youth

by Billy Childish

£7.95UK • $19.95AUS • Not available in the USA • ISBN: 1 899598 08 1

Highly personal and uncompromising, *Notebooks of a Naked Youth* is narrated by one William Loveday, an acned youth possessed of piercing intelligence, acute self-loathing and great personal charm. Haunted by intense sexual desires, the ghosts of his childhood and a 7000 year old mummified Bog Man, William Loveday leads us on a naked odyssey from the 'Rust Belt' of North Kent to the sleazy sex clubs of Hamburg's Reeperbahn – a twilight world of murderous pimps and tattooed hermaphrodites – and a final descent into an expressionist hell.

   In this, his 'fantastic biography', Billy Childish achieves the unholy union of punk rock, Knut Hamsun and Céline. The result is a hilarious, drunken, un-English voyage into the human shadow.

'A seething, dyslexic, better-looking British Bukowski'
– The Observer

CODEX

www.codex-books.com

Neighbourhood Threat: On Tour With Iggy Pop

by Alvin Gibbs

£12.95UK • $19.95USA • $29.95AUS/CAN • With 50 b/w photos • ISBN: 1 899598 17 0

A rock biography with a difference, *Neighbourhood Threat: On Tour With Iggy Pop* is Alvin Gibbs's account of playing bass on a world tour with Iggy Pop.

Neighbourhood Threat features drugs, booze and professional Japanese groupies. Follow Iggy round the globe as he suffers stage fright in front of David Bowie, and single-handedly takes on Pepsi Cola. Meanwhile, his band members experience vomiting while Johnny Thunders of the New York Dolls has sex on the other side of the bathroom, and a Guns N' Roses party that takes on Sadeian proportions.

Alvin Gibbs has been a performing and recording musician since the punk explosion of the late seventies, working with a number of bands, most notably the UK Subs. He is the author of *Destroy: The Definitive History of Punk Rock*, has recently completed a film screenplay, and is working on a novel.

'Iggy Pop and Alvin Gibbs are two cool ass motherfuckers, and this is one cool ass book' – Metal Hammer

'Gibbs retells the carnage with a steady and engrossing eye for detail' – Bizarre

CODEX

www.codex-books.com

Cobralingus

by Jeff Noon

£9.95UK • $14.95USA • $24.95AUS/CAN • ISBN: 1 899598 16 2

Illustrated by Daniel Allington • Introduction by Michael Bracewell

Cobralingus is a literary revolution. It explores new ways of creating stories, using only imaginary technologies and the strangely twisted pathways inside Jeff Noon's head.

Jeff Noon transforms techniques from dance music into a new approach to the production of words. He begins with his own fiction, or 'samples' from Shakespeare, Thomas De Quincy or Zane Grey. These are playfully 'remixed' by the Cobralingus Engine, producing fiction, poems, songs and visually stunning text.

The Cobralingus Engine was first used in Jeff Noon's most recent novel, the critically acclaimed *Needle in the Groove*. His other novels are *Automated Alice*, *Nymphomation, Vurt* and *Pollen*. He has also published *Pixel Juice*, a collection of short stories.

'A virtuoso performance' – The Big Issue

'Noon's language is infected by a dream-bright surrealism' – Rain Taxi

<www.cobralingus.com>

www.codex-books.com

Junk DNA

by Tania Glyde

£7.95uk • $12.95usa • $19.95aus/can • ISBN: 1 899598 19 7

In a world about to be turned upside down by the Human Genome Project, unconventional sex therapist Regina treats her women clients with stolen pharmaceuticals. Bizarrely, they all develop a terrifying aversion to children. Disillusioned, she embarks on a satirical, living exhibition of genetic poetry, starting with mice and working up the evolutionary scale.

Lucy, Regina's ten-year-old neighbour, is a dyslexic, creative genius, born into a family on the wrong side of dysfunctional. As society starts to fall apart, Lucy quits school, orphans herself, and sets to work as Regina's assistant. Lucy becomes a very powerful little girl, and life gets more twisted by the day.

Tania Glyde is the author of *Clever Girl* and features in the *Disco 2000* and *Vox 'N' Roll* anthologies.

'Gleefully dark satire' – Nova

'Junk DNA is energetic, explosive and strangely fascinating. The literary equivalent of a Manga movie' – The Big Issue in the North

www.codex-books.com

Crucify Me Again

by Mark Manning

£8.95UK • $14.50USA • $22.95AUS/CAN • ISBN: 1 899598 14 6
Illustrated by the author

For a decade Mark Manning was Zodiac Mindwarp, sex god, love machine from outer space and frontman of heavy metal band The Love Reaction. *Crucify Me Again* documents the spiralling depravity of his years within the moral quagmire of bad sex, worse drugs and truly horrific rock and roll. Presenting a vivid series of incidents from his life, Mark Manning explores parts of his psyche most people would rather believe didn't exist.

Mark Manning has worked extensively with fellow adventurer, Bill Drummond of The KLF. The pair have co-authored *Bad Wisdom* and published the near mythical elephant folio *A Bible of Dreams*. Currently they collaborate to produce the 'Bad Advice' column for *The Idler*.

'Tales of excess and bravado imbued with a self-deprecating wit' – The Guardian

CODEX

www.codex-books.com

CHARLIEUNCLENORFOLKTANGO

by Tony White

£7.95UK • $11.95USA • $19.95AUS/CAN • ISBN: 1 899598 13 8

CHARLIEUNCLENORFOLKTANGO is a 'stream-of-sentience' alien abduction cop novel, the bastard offspring of *Starsky And Hutch* and *The X Files*.

　　CHARLIEUNCLENORFOLKTANGO is the call sign of three English cops driving around in a riot van. Problem is, one of *these* cops is not entirely human. The Sarge thinks it's him, and Lockie – the narrator – thinks he's right. Well it can't be that dozy tosspot Blakie, can it? In between witnessing and committing various atrocities and acts of work-a-day corruption, *and* being experimented on by aliens, Lockie thinks aloud about old Blakie and The Sarge, cave blokes and cave birds, Charlie's Angels, and "the kynd a fingz that blokes & birds do to keep the dark dark nyte at bay."

　　Tony White lives in London. He is the author of *Road Rage* and *Satan! Satan! Satan!* and edited the *britpulp!* anthology. He is currently literary editor of *The Idler*.

'Utterly brutal, darkly hilarious – the most remarkable novel of alien abduction I've ever read' – Front

CODEX

www.codex-books.com

Digital Leatherette

by Steve Beard

£8.95UK • $14.50USA • $22.95AUS/CAN • ISBN: 1 899598 12 X

The ultimate London cyberpunk novel. A surrealist narrative of text fragments pulled down from invented internet websites by an imaginary intelligence agent.

Digital Leatherette is a London cyberpunk novel featuring the Rave at the End of the World in Battersea Power Station, UFOs over Heathrow, street riots sponsored by fashion designers, MI6 agents running their own reality cop shows, a stock market crash triggered by a star in the sky, a dangerous new drug called Starflower and barcode tattoos.

Steve Beard is the author of a novella *Perfumed Head,* and a collection of essays and journalism, *Logic Bomb: Transmissions from the Edge of Style Culture.*

'An exuberant, neurologically-specific, neo-Blakeian riff-collage. I enjoyed it enormously' – William Gibson

www.codex-books.com

Confusion Incorporated:
A Collection Of Lies, Hoaxes & Hidden Truths

by Stewart Home

£7.95UK • $11.95USA • $19.95AUS/CAN • ISBN: 1 899598 11 1

Confusion Incorporated brings together, for the first time, the hilarious journalistic deceptions of arch wind-up merchant Stewart Home. The imaginative, the complicated, the subtle, the funny – the very, very funny – comprise the subject matter of this compendium of Home's magazine articles and lectures. Regardless of whether Home is being crude, rude or devious, he hits his targets with deadly accuracy and side-splitting effect.

Stewart Home is the author of numerous books including *Cunt, The Assault on Culture, The Mind Invaders* and *Come Before Christ & Murder Love*. He has contributed journalism to an astonishing range of newspapers, magazines and fanzines.

'Quick, funny – the outrageous pieces leap off the page with manic energy' – Time Out

www.codex-books.com

Cranked Up Really High

by Stewart Home

£5.95UK • $9.50USA • $14.95AUS/CAN • ISBN: 1 899598 01 4

A lot of ink has been spilt on the subject of punk rock in recent years, most of it by arty-farty trendies who want to make the music intellectually respectable. *Cranked Up Really High* is different. It isn't published by a university press and it gives short shrift to the idea that the roots of punk rock can be traced back to '*avant garde*' art movements.

As well as discussing sixties garage rock and the British, American and Finnish punk scenes, Home devotes whole chapters to deconstructing Riot Grrl, Oi! and the sorry saga of Nazi bonehead band Skrewdriver. This book champions the super-dumb sleazebag thud of The Ramones, The Stooges, The Vibrators, The Art Attacks, The Snivelling Shits, The Lurkers, The Queers, The Germs, The Child Molesters, The Ants and The Blaggers.

'A complex, provocative book which deserves to be read' – Mojo

See our half price offer on the back page...

Codex books are available in good bookshops worldwide and from internet bookstores.

To order by mail, send a cheque, postal order or International Money Order (payable to CODEX BOOKS, in UK Pounds, drawn on a British bank) to
Codex Books, PO Box 148, Hove, BN3 3DQ, UK.

Postage is free in the UK, add £1 per item for Europe, £2 for the rest of the world. Send a stamp (UK) or International Reply Coupon for a catalogue.

CODEX BOOKS QUESTIONNAIRE

Fill in this short questionnaire (photocopies are acceptable)
and get one of the books listed in the preceding pages at
HALF PRICE!

Name:

Address:

Post Code:

Country:

Email:

Where did you buy this book?

List any other Codex books that you have purchased:

Would you like to be on a Codex Books mailing list? YES☐ NO☐

Would you like to be on a Codex Books email list? YES☐ NO☐

ORDER FORM (first book half price)	
title	price
Postage UK: free • Europe: £1 per book • World: £2 per book	
Total:	

Send a cheque, postal order or International Money Order (payable
to CODEX BOOKS, in UK Pounds, drawn on a British bank) to
Codex Books, PO Box 148, Hove, BN3 3DQ, UK